Washoe Moon, Dorian, Symbiotic
Purple Mist: Strange Novelette Trilogies

By R. Manolakas

ISBN: 978-0-9898545-9-7
LCCN: 2017912653

DEDICATION:

To author Truman Capote, father of the modern crime novel, who receives far too little credit and doesn't deserve it; and to artist Vincent Van Gogh, who receives far too much credit, but does deserve it.

"Stars, hide your fires; let not light see my black and deep desires."

-–Shakespeare's *Macbeth*

FOREWORD

This is the first in a series of spine-tingling, Sci-Fi/Horror, novelette trilogies specifically written for audiobooks as well as e-books—and for *binge listening*, as well as *binge reading*. It appears in paperback too. Dramatic punch and character richness aren't drowned in oceans of exposition and backstory. Hopefully, you'll get that *Outer Limits* feeling—with a little more tooth—and a quicker dramatic payoff than with standard, longer novels.

In the plot of our first of three original stories a family vacations at a secluded mountain cabin beside a reputedly bottomless lake, and instead of enjoying a charming reunion on Thanksgiving weekend, it's plunged into a horrific battle for survival. Next, we encounter a fastidious and talented young man who happens upon a very strange hyperlink that none of us would want to click on. In the last, set in 1919 Utah, a mysterious female doctor introduces a new treatment to the skeptical citizens of a small, isolated town—the cure in this case being far worse than the disease.

Each of the three novelettes is roughly a third the size of a full-length novel, and each is divided into three parts at major plot points—very convenient places to pause if you wish. Each novelette is told in the *present t*ense—for immediacy of experience—like screenplays. This *innovative structuring* is intended to *maximize entertainment per unit of time invested,* and is ideal for your Audible app-enabled smartphone or Kindle and busy, multitasking lifestyle.

One word of advice, please don't listen to or read the Afterword before the entire book, since spoilers may be present.

Twilight Zone, One Step Beyond, and other eerie, TV fare delved into the unexpected and the deliciously disturbing subconscious, and the hope here is that you'll get more of the same. In the following pages, you'll be presented one novelette that is set in the past, one in the present, and another in the future—in different locals. This adds variety and scope to the book, and ties into the theme that time is both fluid and an integral character of the plotline.

May the purple mist of life touch you in a good way and that you enjoy listening to and reading this flagship book, the first in a series of handy and strange little novels. I trust that your audiobook experience on Audible.com will be a satisfying one. If you enjoy the book, please consider writing an online review on the Amazon or Audible site.

Thank you; and good listening—and reading!

R. Manolakas

September 2017

Washoe Moon
Novelette One
Part One

In Washoe County Nevada, it isn't far from Reno to the Shoanah Indian Reservation near Lake Tahoe, but to Sylvia Crawler, the visiting nurse assigned to the Indian Health Service, the drive seems like an eternity.

Her new Subaru Forrester navigates the hairpin turns at a crawl, first up the granite, tree-studded mountains and then down, plunging her into both exhilaration and apprehension. It's exhilaration because of the bonding with her heritage, and apprehension because of the potential evil that accompanies it—like death hitching a lethal ride.

She feels this country in her bones, its beauty enchanting. Yet, she mulls what dragged her back home—one year ago exactly—from Irvine, California to this land with the "bottomless lake." A widow, she fought her headstrong kids—except for her precious Ben—to make the move, and they're still fighting it.

Was it really the beauty of the Sierra Nevadas? Or was it rather the unspeakable horror that had engulfed her ancestors one hundred and fifty years ago that brought her back? As Sylvia descends, navigating the last turn, a huge hunk of blue shimmers through the right passenger window from thousands of feet down—past the narrow road's guardrail.

It's Lake Tahoe! I'm back here at last, she says to herself.

She must be careful driving this treacherous highway, since, although it's been a relatively warm, clear, late November so far, the black ice still poses a threat at that vaunting altitude. A brown-and-white sign—rimmed by buckskin—heralds the motorist: TURNOFF FOR INDIAN HEALTH SERVICE AND SHOANAH INDIAN RESERVATION.

Winding her way into the large valley, she braces as she reads the second road-sign, the one that had always—as a young girl—wedged a lump in her throat: TURNOFF TO THE CRAWLER PARTY CAMPSITE—NEXT LEFT.

Being late for her first appointment, she speeds up and continues straight ahead, bypassing the site of the old Crawler shack where the legend started. The Indian clinic soon comes into view. It's been many years since she visited the old reservation, since grade school, in fact. At the entrance to a log cabin stands the tall, rail-thin figure of Tom Redfern—the administrator of the Health Service and Chief of the Shoanah Tribe.

His silver-filled, canine tooth reflects in the midday sun as he smiles widely, waving at her. Sylvia is familiar with that gleam of metal, since she also has a gold-filled incisor in her bottom row of teeth. It too, she's been told, can reflect light when she smiles.

"Welcome Nurse Crawler. I've been looking forward to this," says Chief Redfern, "it's not every day that we have a celebrity."

Sylvia, having an idea of what he's referring to and not sure that she likes it, closes the car door. This man with the moccasins, black shirt and slacks, salt and-pepper ponytail, and piercing, dark eyes escorts her into the clinic. His voice is smooth and low.

"Let's sit here at my desk and chat a bit, shall we? It's your first day here. So, let's go over some ground rules."

He covers all the material that had been mentioned in her acceptance letter. She notices the beaded necklace hanging from his neck, marked with tribal designs.

"I hear my first patient is a hundred-year-old member of your tribe—a Medicine Man, so to speak," says Sylvia, getting right down to business. "He has a chest cold."

She looks around the clinic, noting a few Western oil paintings, replete with buffalo, and horseback-Indians chasing them with feathers in their hair. Wolf skins hang on the knotty-pine paneled walls, and the doors of the two exam rooms on the other side of the structure—each with a chart-rack at their entrance—are positioned next to the bathroom.

"I chose your application, Ms. Redfern, because you have roots here," says the Chief as he sits in his fur-lined easy chair behind his antique, redwood desk. "That's important."

Sylvia, preferring that she be picked for her experience and training, can understand his preference. The Shoanah tribe has very special healthcare needs, which a nurse must recognize. She laments that the tribe seems to have a real problem with alcohol from what she read on the job description. That means liver problems, for one.

Sylvia likes the look of the place, which isn't without its rustic, ethnic charm. A huge fireplace roars opposite them. Over the fire hangs an old, group photograph of some three hundred or so settlers gathered around a Conestoga wagon. A young woman sits at the reins. Like the other trekkers, she wears a cowboy hat and looks into the camera over the backs of her team of horses.

Sylvia's eyes freeze on the woman. She grips the armrest of her chair.

Tom Redfern's black eyes, embedded in wrinkles from years in the sun, dart from his guest to the photo. "I see you recognize the resemblance. Yes, that's a picture of the Crawler Party, circa eighteen-sixty seven." Sylvia notices again the glint of reflecting firelight from Redfern's tooth. "That woman sitting at the helm of the wagon is also Sylvia Crawler—"

"Yes, I know," says the visiting nurse, "I've seen it before." She had almost forgotten the grainy, black and white photograph that actually had made its way into more than one history book. She never got used to the shock of seeing it. She wonders why Redfern, of all people, would memorialize a photo like that.

"Of course," he responds with a tight smile, revealing yellow teeth. "I'm sure you have."

Sylvia notices that the woman's jaw in the photo is squared like hers, her large eyes light colored and intense, and her nose turned up and freckled, also just like hers. Like her too, the mouth is wide and thin-lipped and the body sturdy.

"She's my great, great—something or other—grandmother—"

"That's evident, Ms. Crawler."

"You know, you don't talk how I expected a tribal chief to talk—" Sylvia stops abruptly, realizing the stereotyped nature of her remark.

Redfern chuckles, but his face is serious. "I hear that quite often. I graduated from Yale."

"And you came back here? That's commendable."

"Not at all. This place is very special. Much more than you may realize."

"Yes, it must be," responds Sylvia. Her eyes shift from the photo to a skull resting upon Redfern's desk. She realizes that it's a human skull—and it unnerves her, interrupting her train of thought . . .

"I see you're staring at my heirloom—a souvenir from the Crawler Party. It's rumored to belong to the best friend of the wagon master—Josiah Crawler, Sylvia's husband."

Sylvia's glare meets his stare. *Why is this strange man going into all this,* she wonders. *What would motivate him to keep such a gruesome thing in his office?* Oh well, she figures, the Shoanah do have their ways about them.

The room is hot, the small, closed windows not releasing the heat from the fireplace. Sylvia feels herself sweating into her pristine, white nurse's uniform. Uncomfortable, she rises to her feet. "Chief Redfern, please tell me about the first patient. " She looks at her watch. " It's nearly time for the appointment."

Redfern rises, shaking his head, "I do apologize. Call me *Tom*," he says in a flat voice as he walks around the desk to stand very close to her. He peers into her eyes. "I didn't mean to upset you." His eyes roam her person, making her a bit uncomfortable. Also, the twinkle in his gaze suggests to Sylvia that this man just might be playing with her a bit.

"I'm not upset in the least," shoots back Sylvia, "on the contrary, it's very interesting. I've been living with the folklore of the Crawler Party all my life."

"'Folklore' you say?" he practically whispers, his eyes also betraying a trace of menace. "After your kin got stuck in the pass, a rescue party came out here from Reno. That was the start of a flood of white settlers here. Your name is very well known. Welcome home, Ms. Crawler."

"Tell me more about the first patient."

"His name is 'Black-Tongue'" says Redfern. "He's waiting in the exam room now. He might resent you—after all—he *is* a Medicine Man from the *old* school. You'll find him very *interesting* too, I'm sure. Just go through his chart." Redfern points to the closest exam room, its door open a crack, and the patient's medical record perched on the wall.

Sylvia glances at the skull. She has an odd feeling. What Tom Redfern doesn't know is that she suspects that her ancestry did indeed compel her return to her roots in Nevada. She doesn't know why, and she would never admit that in a million years.

Her mind sticks on one thought, one that indulges in a bit of white-settler cliché. As she ambles to the exam room, she can't get around the notion that her appointment to work at the clinic had not been entirely due to her sterling credentials.

There's more to it than that. The whole thing will play out in the end the way it's meant to.

Is there some sort of Indian revenge lying at the bottom of all this?

* * *

"You good white woman. Bring white man's medicine. I die soon."

"For a chest cold?" says Sylvia to the wrinkled, ancient looking old man, "I can do better than that."

She smiles, looking up from her stool to the exam table, where the Shoanah Medicine Man sits, his tan, buckskin trousers and shirt separated by a brightly decorated tribal belt. "Unbutton your shirt at the top please, Mr.—"

"Call me Black-Tongue," he says with a barely audible, scratchy voice. His bony, wizened fingers fumble with his buttons made of deer bone.

Sylvia stands up and leans toward her patient, inserting the head of her stethoscope into the opening of his shirt, reaching her hand around his slight chest to auscultate the back of his torso. She notices his lovely turquoise necklace and the gamy, smoky scent of his thinning, white hair.

"Your lungs are clear."

She removes her instrument and takes her ophthalmoscope out of her blouse pocket, then examines the fundi of the patient's eyes. "Within normal limits. I just can't seem to find anything wrong with you, sir. You're too healthy! Not bad for one hundred and one."

The patient peers into her eyes. Sylvia can see that the man's golden eyes—slits really in a sea of wrinkles—are focusing on *her* left eye. She feels that he's studying the dark inclusion at the rim of her left iris at the three o'clock position, a rare, familial birthmark that's hard to miss at close quarters.

"I see little black stone on edge of blue lake," utters the patient.

"Oh yes. My eighteen-year-old daughter—also named Sylvia—has one too. It's a family thing. What we call in the trade a familial birthmark."

"I am sad for you," he rejoined.

Sylvia, uncomfortable with this stranger commenting on the flaw in her otherwise flawless blue eyes, changes the subject. She stands straight, looking him in the eye, her hands on her hips, putting the instrument back in her pocket.

"Just why did you want to see the nurse today, Black-Tongue?" Sylvia could feel—just like she had with Tom Redfern—a hidden agenda.

The old man frowns, then reaches into his pocket and hands her a small piece of Indian art made of dark blue and white beads. "This is for you," he says.

She takes the strange object in her hands. Sylvia sees a flat, oval decoration with a small white circle on a dark background. It has a musty smell. "The moon?" she asks.

"You are wise. Yes, the moon. You come back here—to find your fate. The moon will die. The white woman with the black stone in her eye will not rest."

Sylvia gives him back his gift. "I'm not sure I should keep this, but thank you anyway." She backs up from her strange patient. She doesn't know whether to laugh or to cry. "I don't understand these things, Black-Tongue. Just how do you know all this?"

Somehow, she feels that this gift is a warning.

Black-Tongue's eyes widen. "*All* my people know; wood in fire makes smoke. Out of this, pictures come. Pictures teach me, and my people. They make us well. Others, not so good."

Sylvia takes a seat behind the desk in the corner, charting her medical notes. "I'll treat you symptomatically. You may have an early flu. I'll prescribe you acyclovir. Take it as directed."

Tears run down the old man's cheek. He shakes his head, the coarse hair falling to his shoulders. "Leave this place. Go. Before . . . "

Sylvia, rather than consoling the distraught patient, heads for the door. She's had enough. When she places her hand on the knob, she notices her fingers shaking.

"You can get fully dressed now. They'll give you your medicine on the way out. I'll see you back in one month." She closes the door too hastily to hear the last comment from the old Medicine Man.

"No, you will not."

Sylvia rushes to the bathroom. She strides to the mirror. She peers into it, examining the small dot at the rim of her left sclera. She frowns, and then unbuttons her blouse, opening it to reveal the anterior aspect of her bare left shoulder.

There it is. The same pattern exactly!

Sylvia's looking at the large tattoo she had received long ago—after a teenage bout of drunkenness—in a seedy parlor.

It's the same!

She had never understood why or how that particular design had been chosen. She only remembers that the artist had described himself as "a half-breed Indian."

Sylvia swallows hard. Her eyes are fastened on the image in the tattoo: a small white circle on an oval, dark blue background.

* * *

Sylvia's Reno apartment is three bedrooms and ample size, but it still feels very cramped with her four children. She sits around the kitchen table at suppertime, with her two boys and two girls. They gobble hot dogs, baked beans, coleslaw, and cherry pie fresh from the bakery. Songs from the Beach Boys play in the background from an old, cordless, battery-charged CD player resting on the dirty, beige counter. The kitchen is separated from the living room by a small partition.

Their home is Spartan, with grey walls, plain light fixtures, prints of the Washoe Valley hanging on the walls, and functional, oak furniture. The tablecloth has a pattern of red roosters and yellow farm-hens.

"Mom—turn off that old-guy music!" begs Sylvia junior, Sylvia's eighteen-year-old daughter and namesake, as she dollops beans on her paper plate. She pushes back the spray of blond bangs from her forehead, "Why *must* we eat on paper plates—?"

"Shut up, quit complaining," snaps Ben in his usual steady voice as he neatly arranges his hotdog fixings on his tidy plate. "You're always griping about something. Besides, the Beach Boys are *boss.*"

"Quiet, both of you!" chides the mother as she reaches for the mustard.

This smart fourteen-year-old, she muses, my oldest son—lording over the family at the head of the table—is a pure Godsend. *Ben is always so even keeled.* He remembers everything, including the lingo from the period of her favorite band. *"Boss"—I haven't heard that word in thirty years. Why can't the rest be more like Ben?*

Daughter Sylvia scowls at Adam. The quiet but cantankerous, finicky four-year-old sticks his tongue out at her as he dabbles with his mess of coleslaw.

Ten-year-old Blythe, the headstrong and impulsive troublemaker, sits over an empty plate next to Adam. She quickly pinches her little brother's nose in the cleft between her middle and index finger, and then shows him what she caught—her thumb protruding between her knuckles. "See, I got your nose—"

"No! That's your thumb," corrects Adam. He snorts a laugh.

The mother looks on as they play their game. Sylvia is home-schooling Adam, who is wise beyond his years. She intends to enroll him in next year's kindergarten class for gifted pupils, that is, if he can overcome his behavioral issues.

"You all eat your food. Then it's homework time. No TV—"

"But mom," protests Blythe, "I'm done with my homework!"

"Good then," she retorts, "do some more. You could be a little more cooperative, young lady."

Sylvia glances around at her children, whom she regards as an interesting study in genetics. Daughter Sylvia is tall, fair, blue eyed and broad boned like her. Two are slight, dark, and brown eyed, resembling her ex-husband. Ben is the exception—he's an apparent attempt by nature to make sure both parents were represented. His brown hair and blue eyes, and a tall, lanky frame, support this contention. Sylvia had divorced three years before. After the separation, Sylvia chose for her and her children to revert to her maiden name of "Crawler."

"How'd work go, mom?" asks Ben, always the thoughtful one.

"All right, I suppose. You know, the old Crawler cabin is located within the Shoanah Indian property, not far from the lake. There's one other cabin next to it. The two plots were deeded to the white settlers before the government ceded a small portion of the area to the tribe—about a hundred years ago. They used to roam much more—"

"I know, you already told us that," says daughter Sylvia. "Many times."

"Did I? I'm sorry. Well, the cabin's very secluded, but *nice*, according to the realtor. I figure we all go up there and enjoy the peace and quiet. Smartphones and laptops stay in the car trunk—locked up. I want us all to bond—"

"They say that part of the lake is so deep they never found the bottom to it," interjects Ben. "Wow, that's creepy."

Sylvia knows that to be true. The lake is deep, and some parts bottomless. Maybe someday, with the new technology and those little submarines, they'll find it.

"Next weekend is Thanksgiving weekend," she announces. " The realtor says that the old cabin's been refurbished and cleaned. The tribe just put it up for rent—but Chief Redfern promised me first dibs. I'd like us to spend the holiday there, from Friday evening to Sunday evening."

Sylvia looks around the table at her children. If she had let off a stink bomb, the reaction couldn't have been more negative: scowls—and dead silence. Blythe casts her eyes down to the table.

"I want us to feel," she continues wistfully, "a connection with our forebears. I feel we owe it to them after the terrible things that happened there."

What Sylvia doesn't mention is that she has always felt an uncanny desire to be drawn back to the site of the Crawler disaster, as if an invisible hand were grabbing her by the neck and dragging her to that infamous cabin by the lake.

"But mom, I don't want to stay in that stinky old cabin—" says Sylvia.

"Me too," says Adam. "I want turkey *here*."

"We'll have our Thanksgiving in Reno, honey," reassures Sylvia. "It's the Thursday before."

"That Crawler stuff gives me the willies," chimes in Blythe. "They say those people froze, or starved to death, and ate each other. Isn't that a crime, Mother?"

"I know what they say young lady!" All of a sudden, the harmonizing tune in the background seems oddly out of place to Sylvia, considering the grim content of the conversation. "That was a hundred and fifty years ago!"

Feeling a rush of anxiety coming over her, Sylvia digs into the pocket of her apron, and then remembers that she quit smoking the year before. "I don't want to hear any more talk like that, do you understand me Blythe Crawler?"

"I'll say what I like," Blythe shoots back. "They ate their horses, too—"

"Leave the table this instant!"

Blythe just sits there, ignoring her mother, playing with her plastic fork. "All right. I'll be good."

Sylvia looks plaintively at Ben.

Her dutiful son looks up from his plate, and shrugs. "I'm with you mom. If it means that much to you, let's do it—"

"Well I'm *not* with you!" retorts the oldest daughter. "I've got *plans*, anyway. Why did we have to leave Irvine for this rat-hole in the first place?" Sylvia glares at her mother. "You dragged us out here. And now I have to spend my vacation at some creepy Indian dump!"

The mother jumps up from the table, glaring at her kids. She starts emptying the table of plates and plastic utensils. "We're going and that's it! I've already put down a deposit. It's only two days, for Christ's sake!" She throws the plates in the trash. "That's settled. Go do your homework."

The children get up from the table and empty out into the bedrooms—all except Ben, who lingers quietly, his gentle gaze fixed on his mother. "You OK, mom?"

Sylvia turns toward her son, her eyes meeting his. "I think so, honey." She places her hand gently upon his shoulder.

"I hope I didn't make a mistake coming back here."

* * *

After she makes sure all her children are tucked in, Sylvia slips into her king-sized bed with the brown and white quilts and beige, Egyptian cotton sheets. She looks around her bedroom with pride.

She had decorated it well, but not too good since, in the fall, she plans to move the family into a house. Maplewood dressers, a walnut bed-stand, and an antique rocker complement the Swiss coffee-colored walls, from which hang wood-carved ornaments with an Old West flare. A TV screen on a stand, and a radio on the shelf, round out her bedroom appointments.

She props up her pillows and turns on the reading light sitting on the bed-stand, then flicks off the light fixture hanging overhead. The rain pings hard against the picture widow across the room. The wind howls, and Sylvia can feel the temperature falling in her room, despite the thermostat being set to seventy-four.

She gets up from her bed and walks over to the window, opening the curtains, peering into the darkness that, during the day, reveals a beautiful meadow. Presently, she observes the rain turn into sleet, pounding the glass even harder.

Is there a big storm brewing, she wonders?

Sylvia goes over to her closed door and locks it. She ambles to the dresser and removes an old, dusty, hardcover book. She takes it back to bed with her.

Legends of the Old West has a strange, briny smell, but she leafs through the yellowed pages anyway, stopping on the third chapter: "The Tragedy of the Crawler Party."

On the first page of the chapter, she sees the same old photograph that she saw in Tom Redfern's office just two days before. Skimming through the chapter more, she spots a reproduction of a period newspaper item, presented in block print. She whispers the passage to herself:

"DATELINE DECEMBER 13, 1867—SAN FRANCISCO CHRONICLE—

THE UNFORTUNATE "CRAWLER PARTY"—THREE HUNDRED SOULS TREKKING BY COVERED WAGON FROM KANSAS TO CALIFORNIA THROUGH A PASS IN THE SIERRA NEVADAS—WAS CAUGHT IN A FREAK SNOWSTORM TWO DAYS AFTER THANKSGIVING, ON NOVEMBER 25th, IN NORTHERN NEVADA.

THE HAPLESS SETTLERS MISSED TRAVERSING THE OPEN PASS BY ONLY THREE HOURS! FORCED TO TURN BACK, THEY FOUND SHELTER IN A SMALL CABIN NEAR TAHOE, A HUGE, DEEP LAKE WHICH ALMOST FROZE SOLID COMPLETELY FOR THE FIRST TIME IN MEMORY. THE BRAVE PIONEERS BATTLED FROSTBITE AND STARVATION.

A RESCUE PARTY THAT REACHED THE CABIN TWO WEEKS AFTER THE STORM ABATED WERE SHOCKED TO UNCOVER EVIDENCE OF GODLESS CANNABILISM. TWO SETTLERS SURVIVED THE ORDEAL: THE WAGON MASTER—JOSIAH CRAWLER—AND HIS YOUNG WIFE SYLVIA. ONE OF THEIR FOUR CHILDREN IS SAID TO HAVE SURVIVED ALSO. BY STRANGE COINCIDENCE, THE ONSET OF THE SNOWSTORM CAME DURING A RARE, LUNAR FULL-ECLIPSE.

FANTISTACILLY, ONE SPOKESMAN IN THE RESCUE PARTY CLAIMS THAT A LOCAL SHOANAH INDIAN BRAVE—HELPING TO DIG OUT THE VICTIMS FROM THE BURIED CABIN—INFORMED THEM THAT THIS TRAGEDY REPRESENTS A TRIBAL CURSE— EMPOWERED BY THE LUNAR EVENT—AS PUNISHMENT FOR TRESSPASING ON THE LAND OF THE SAVAGES!"

FURHTER DETIALS WILL BE FORTHCOMING."

Sylvia, her eyes wide as saucers, slams the book shut and throws it into the drawer of her bed stand, like its a contaminated bandage. She hears the wind howling even louder, and the glass being pounded by even bigger sleet. She fears the window will shatter.

She takes the remote off the stand, and turns on the TV to the local Weather Channel. The anchorwoman points to a map of the Tahoe area.

She warns: " . . . Get ready for a huge snowstorm this Thanksgiving weekend in the area of the Shoanah reservation. We project that it will hit Monday morning. This is very unusual weather for so early in the snow season. That's not all. *There'll be a very rare, complete, lunar eclipse on Saturday evening!* Our chief meteorologist tells us that this is the first such eclipse since eighteen sixty-seven. We'll keep you posted . . . "

Sylvia flicks off the TV.

She buries herself under her covers. At least, she figures, the big storm won't hit until Monday, and they'll be gone Sunday. She doesn't mind the modest element of risk. It's a challenge, and she'll meet it just like her sturdy forebears did. Her mind races: *this Indian mumbo jumbo can't all be true!*

The real question running through her mind is: do I chuck the damn nursing gig and get the hell out of Nevada with my kids?

Or, do I face my heritage and see what fate deals me?

To Sylvia Crawler, the answer was never really in doubt.

* * *

Sylvia and the kids pull up to the old Crawler Cabin late Friday afternoon, the beginning of the Thanksgiving Day weekend being bright but windy. The day before, the family had feasted on Turkey with all the fixings at the Circus-Circus Casino in downtown Reno, near their apartment.

Sylvia had been too tired and nervous to cook, a chore that she didn't relish. In fact, their food supply for their little retreat—stuffed in the rear cargo area of the Forrester—consists of cans of baked beans, Dennison's chili, and Costco chocolate chip cookies—replete with plastic utensils, linens, toilet paper, soda-pop, and other miscellaneous items.

She had obtained the key to the massive, oaken front door of the log cabin from the realtor, which she removes from her glove box. Sylvia and the kids get out of the car. With her brood in tow, she slowly approaches the long, wrap-around porch, noticing that some of the wooden planks have rotted just below the flimsy structure's small window.

Although refurbished, it's nevertheless disappointedly rundown. Relieved, she realizes that the little storm had cleared the day before, and the big one was still projected for Monday, when they will already be gone. If the place blows down, at least they won't be in the middle of it.

The mostly clear sky, a lovely ultramarine blue with a dash of burnt orange and violet, is a sharp contrast to the ugly cabin. Of course, no phone lines lead to the structure. And, as the realtor had advised her, there's no electricity in the cabin either—just kerosene lanterns and a ground-floor fireplace. Sylvia, however, secretly welcomes this throwback to old times.

She notices a sliver of blue lake through the huge, swaying pines, just below a tree-lined trail, about a quarter mile off. Another trail leads off to what looks like the corner of another cabin, about a hundred yards away, slightly above theirs. This must be the odd neighbor Barnes, she figures. She points to the small, log-lined structure just below their cabin and to the side of the porch, with a narrow door. "That must be the woodshed," she explains to the others.

Sylvia leads her brood up the rickety, half-log steps. "Be careful climbing these stairs and walking around on the porch. They don't feel none too sturdy," she warns her brood. She's surprised, however, by how large and sprawling the old place is, much larger than the original structure she remembers as a girl. The pinewood add-ons, nevertheless, look slapdash and out of place, especially the second story—which includes what looks like a gabled attic.

Apparently, she muses condescendingly, the Indians had a hand in this renovation.

Little Adam, like the others, wears a citified variation of Levis, sneakers, and a Parka, with a woolen ski-cap of bright yellow—with Ben wearing a red one. Adam darts up the stairs to the porch despite his mother's warning.

"I *said*, be careful!" she admonishes as the family approaches the front door. Sylvia sees her eldest daughter clutching her smartphone. "You give me that phone. I told *all* of you—no laptops or phones until Monday! That includes *you*, Sylvia. For once, I want peace and quiet—and none of this digital crap!"

Sylvia, regretting her profanity, confiscates the phone, and then notices Blythe tucking her phone into her yellow ski jacket. "That one too. Hand it over!"

Sylvia knows that Ben already has deposited his laptop in the trunk of the car. Scrappy Ben has rough edges but he obeys her, she mulls thankfully. Despite several fistfights at school—which he had handily won—he's always been a good and steadfast boy, and a tolerable student as well. She holds up her car keys, glaring at her children. "These gismos are locked up in the car until we leave. Only *I* have the key."

She proceeds to do just that, placing the confiscated phones in the back of the vehicle, and then locking the car. She ambles back up to the front door, noticing another trail that winds into the dense forest. She remembers that the trail leads to the center of the Indian reservation—known as the "Indian Village"—about a mile due east.

The wooden plank creaks as she plants herself in front of the solid front door, bolted shut by a padlocked, fastened to a thicker slab of wood. She places the key into the dusty, rusted lock.

"OK gang," she says with some sense of foreboding, "let's go in."

* * *

After bolting the front door behind them, Sylvia surveys the interior of the cabin with Ben, while the other children store the supplies in the kitchen pantry, griping about how cold it is in the cabin.

She starts at the bottom floor, which is one huge room. The fireplace and piled kindling are positioned at one wall, under the huge brick chimney that can be seen running up the ten-foot wall. Ben sticks his shaggy head into the fireplace and looks up, and then whistles. "Wow mom, this thing's big enough to crawl up all the way to the roof!"

"It has to be," adds Sylvia. "Winters can be pretty cold up here. In fact, it's getting cold in here *now*. After we look around a bit, take that wood and the lighter fluid in the kitchen and start a fire."

Ben smiles and nods good-naturedly. He's always up for doing his chores, and does a good job too, she muses. It must be his Boy Scout training, thinks Sylvia. *He'll be an Eagle Scout someday.* He's the only one of her children who's interested in hunting too—mostly birds—and he's damn good at. *Maybe that's why he didn't squawk with the move to Nevada.*

"Mom, look at this shotgun! There's a box of shells on the mantle-piece too." Ben picks the gun off its perch above the fireplace and opens its chamber. "It looks pretty new. I think it's and automatic—oh boy! Big gage, too." He aims the gun at an imaginary bird. "*Boss*—!"

"Careful with that thing!"

"It's not loaded, Mom. I'll load it after supper." Ben then points to a crossbow, which hangs next to the shotgun perch. "I wonder if that thing works. It has arrows too, attached below it."

"Put the gun back," snaps Sylvia. Not a big fan of guns, she nevertheless allows Ben his head on that particular activity. "You can fool with that later. And leave the bow alone—at least for now."

Ben replaces the shotgun. "This rifle needs oiling and cleaning. Crossbow too."

"Ben, take Blythe after supper and clean that dusty sofa over there." Sylvia points to the furniture across the room. "I see cobwebs on the leather easy chair, next to the oak chairs. *I'll* mop the floor."

Sylvia's a bit miffed that the realtor hadn't cleaned the house as much as she promised. The wooden floor is dark with grime and smells like old rags, but no use fretting about that now. She glances over at the other kids. Sylvia junior argues with Blythe.

"What's going on over there?" Sylvia shouts at her daughters.

Blythe—her hands placed on her narrow hips—yells over to her mother from the kitchen. "Mamma, I don't want to clean these stinky old knives—"

"I don't either," shouts daughter Sylvia. "Besides, this old fawcett barely works!" She holds a huge carving knife up to show her mother, "I think there's old blood and some hair on this thing. Yuk! There're others, too." She holds her nose. "Gross!"

"Quit screwing around. Those are probably old game-skinning knives, like grandpa used to own. Do the best you can."

"All right Mamma, anything you say" retorts Blythe as the other daughter tosses the knife into the large, chipped porcelain sink.

"Careful with those things," chides the mother. "And Blythe, I don't want any of your smugness and sarcasm, either! Sylvia, you get the kerosene lamps out of the pantry and see that they have fuel. Place them on the mountings around the cabin." The mother points to one of a series of metal hooks scattered about the room. "Up stairs too. Check out the attic."

Ben ambles over to a small alcove beyond the fireplace, which has a wooden partition. As Sylvia approaches it with her son, it looks to her like a makeshift tool-bin. Within this utility, they see a large hatchet lying on the floor, a hoe, a hammer, and gallon metal containers of kerosene and gasoline. There's also a machete—probably for clearing brush—and some small boards and nails.

"Well," says Sylvia. "Let's have a gander at the upstairs."

She and Ben pass countless old deer skulls and wolf skins festooned about the log-paneled walls as they ascend a wide, creaky stairwell made of steps that are hunks of shaved wood arranged in a half-spiral. "Watch your step, Mom," warns Ben.

Getting to be near sunset, the upstairs is dark and musty, just what Sylvia expected. What she didn't expect is what looks like crusty bloodstains splattered about some of the walls, probably from carrying game loaded with buckshot. She and Ben inspect the long hallway leading to three bedrooms, all overlooking the surrounding forest through small, cedar-lined, bare windows. There's also a bathroom with one of those old fashioned tubs with a shower spigot sticking out of the wall.

Two bedrooms have double bunk beds and one—Sylvia's—is a single. There are no linens, except what they had brought with them, and planks—not soft mattresses—supporting the beds.

"Well," says Sylvia to Ben, " I never said we'd be roughing it."

Ben laughs. "Mom," he says as he points down the dark hall, "there's another small stairway at the end of the hall. That must be the attic. Let's check it out before we get on to the chores."

Ben leads his mother along the dim corridor up to the narrow, steep stairs. They lead to a thick, wooden door, bolted shut. It's unlocked. Ben turns the rusty handle, and then pushes the door open and enters first, with his mother following closely.

"Be careful, Mom, it's dark in here."

Sylvia covers her nose. "It smells like road-kill in this place."

She points to a chink of light coming from above the low-ceilinged, ten-foot-square structure. "Look Ben, a skylight. Almost covered over by God knows what," says Sylvia. "Let's get out of here."

Ben responds by climbing onto the sole chair in the place, and fiddling with the cover of the skylight. He opens it, and examines its lock. "It has a lock on the outside."

All of a sudden, there's a bang on the door. Then, a loud grunt . . .

Ben startles. He jumps down from the chair. "Mama, something's after us! Let's kill it!"

Sylvia moves to the door, pulling it wide open. "Just sister here, playing her games again."

Daughter Sylvia, holding a lantern and canister of kerosene, laughs. "Gotcha!" She steps in a short distance, looking around. "Didn't mean to scare you so; you *said* check out the attic, Mom."

"So I did. Let's get back to the others." On the way out of the creepy enclosure, the mother is able to make out a long narrow object hanging on the wall. She smiles. "Look, a fishing pole! There's a tackle box too."

Sylvia, never an outdoors person, practices one exception to this lifelong avoidance. She loves to fish whenever she can. "Take those with you, Ben. And take the lantern from your sister and leave it in here. Leave the kerosene too, there's another one in the kitchen."

"OK, Mom."

They join the rest of the family downstairs, busily working on their chores. "That realtor said that there's a small rowboat docked down at the lake—for the use of this cabin," mother Sylvia explains on the way. They arrive at the base of the stairwell, next to the kitchen.

"Maybe I'll catch us some dinner tonight at sunset," she adds. "They say Tahoe has some good trout."

"Careful Mom. That's the part of the lake with no bottom to it," offers Blythe—the one with all the facts—as she fuels the remaining lanterns near the pantry.

"Oh, that's what that *Indian* realtor said," sniffs mother Sylvia. "She's the same one who said that this place is *clean*. What does *she* know?"

* * *

"I would've come over and welcomed you to the neighborhood, but my son Blake here needed some help with his studies," chortled Bill Barnes, Professor of Pain Medicine at the University of Nevada at Reno.

The five of them sit around a circular heart—with a funneled hood—leading up to the high ceiling, much higher than in Sylvia's cabin. Bill, his son, Sheriff Naomi Silver-Wolf, and mother Sylvia and daughter Blythe, all recline in their red and white, Indian-embroidered chairs, in front of the crackling flames.

The intense heat feels good on Sylvia's face.

The professor slaps son Blake playfully on his shoulder with his one remaining hand. To Sylvia, the father's pat had a lot more force than was necessary.

"Blake here's trying to get into the medical college at UNR," says Bill, "he's not a quick learner, though, no ma'am," he insists as his shifty eyes dart about the fur-lined living room.

"Oh, I'm sure he'll make out fine," offers Sylvia.

"Imagine that," continues the father, "he wants to be a taxidermist instead, of all things." Professor Barnes points to the various stuffed animals that dot the walls. "With my help, he'll make it into medical school. You bet he will. How about *you*, little girl."

Bill's restless eyes shift to Blythe, who sits next to him. "What do you want to be when you grow up? My son doesn't really know."

Blythe—shy with strangers, looks at her mother, not sure what to say. "Well—"

Sylvia fills the pause. "Blythe is the studious one; straight A's in school. She wants to be a lawyer. Then the FBI—she's a gutsy one all right. Headstrong too."

"*FBI*," gasps Bill incredulously, "you're almost as kooky as my son!"

Sylvia glances at the handsome but gangly son Blake, who rolls his brown eyes in embarrassment. "Get out of here, Pop. Don't tell her *that*—"

The father and son look much alike, muses Sylvia, including their thick, bright-red hair and horn-rimmed eyeglasses. Blake's hair has streaks of green in it, probably his stab at the role of the rebellious son. The major difference in appearance between the two is, however, the loss of the father's left arm, now prosthetic with a metal hook for a hand. According to the realtor, he lost it in Gulf War One.

"Why *not* tell these folks that? It's true. You got my looks and your ma's low intelligence," chortles the professor in a high, nasal voice. "My side of the family had real brains." He winks at little Blythe. "But, Blake can shoot like a fiend. You should see him hunt fox or deer. He's a master at *something*, anyway. He loves to eat his game, too."

Blake looks down at the wooden floor, shaking his head. "Sure Pop, anything you say." He glares at his father with undisguised malice, then his dull eyes shift to Sylvia. "I put some things in you cabin that I think you may need," offers Blake in a soft voice, "hope you don't mind."

Sylvia forces a smile, realizing that the father may not be entirely stable. *Maybe it was the war,* she wonders. She snatches a glance at Silver-Wolf, who's as silent as a stone, staring into the fireplace. "Like what kind of things, Blake? No, of course I don't mind at all."

"Well, I left the gun and the bow. Tell the truth, I've used that cabin a few times for hunting."

He left the shotgun and bow, considers Sylvia, *what an odd thing to do. Why?*

The visiting Sheriff sitting next to Sylvia—Naomi Silver-Wolf—peers out the small, bare window, lost in thought. The burnt orange-splashed glass shows traces of impending sunset. This Indian officer has barely said a word for the whole hour they had been gabbing around the fireplace.

Sylvia studies her. The quiet, young woman is heavy set and wears her jet-black hair in braids. Her high cheekbones, hooked nose, and the narrow cast to her eyes—along with her alizarin-toned skin—suggests she's full blooded Shoanah and not of mixed race, like many in her tribe.

"Tell me Sherriff," says Sylvia, leaning toward Naomi who wears the crisp brown uniform of the tribal officers, "is it true that the lake—in these parts—is *bottomless*?"

Sylvia recalls the realtor mentioning that Officer Silver-Wolf is a crack shot with a high-powered rifle—the best markswoman in Nevada. The young policewoman thinks for a few moments, and then answers in a rote manner as if she's been asked that question a thousand times before.

"It may be so. Some say yes. Some say no. There may be someone who can find the bottom of anything—but no one's tried that here on Indian land."

"Do you know Black-Tongue, the Medicine Man?" asks Sylvia.

At the mention of that name, the eyes of the two Barnes men quickly freeze on Sylvia, as if she just sprouted horns.

Silver-Wolf's black eyes widen in surprise to her question. "What did this crazy man tell you, Sylvia?"

Sylvia didn't expect such an intense reaction. "Oh, just about the legend surrounding the Crawler Party, and things about the moon. Tom Redfern had some interesting comments too. What happened—"?

"Be careful with Black-Tongue," she interrupts. "He asks about you and your family. He wants to visit you at your cabin—soon. Redfern, be careful of him too. Tell me, Sylvia, do you believe in the magic of the legend?"

"I was just going to ask *you* the same question, Sheriff—"

"I don't know," she says as she stares into the fire.

"Well," answers Sylvia, "the history books say the Crawlers did in fact get caught in a snowstorm in eighteen sixty-seven—"

"No," corrects Silver-Wolf, "I mean the *whole* legend?"

"Well, I don't know if I'm privy to the *whole* legend."

Bill Barnes shoots up from his chair and goes to the fireplace, grasping his pipe off the shelf with his hook. "We don't believe all this Indian nonsense. No offense to you, Sherriff. All this about the half-dead tree-people—rising from death—glowing in the night and devouring their friends as they yearn for their spirits to rest in peace, is pure bunk."

He lights the pipe with his good hand, and then returns to his chair and sits down. "It's all garbage; told by a few greedy witnesses in the rescue party who were eager to make a few bucks off the newspapers of the time. Only a fool—"

"What about all the people who have disappeared since," objects Blake? "Sylvia—do you believe what you hear about your distant kin? I don't agree with my dad—"

"Shut up Blake!" Professor Barnes blows his smoke at his son. "Don't rile her any more than she already is. Besides, you're studying to be a doctor, and doctors are scientific men."

His menacing eyes grope his son. He utters irrelevantly, "Blake, bet you can't tell me why I still feel pain in my left hand—the one that's gone."

"And *women*," little Blythe corrects the father, glaring at him. "*Women* are scientists, *too*."

Blake remains silent. Bill glares at the little girl but speaks to his son, answering his own question from the little quiz. "It's called '*phantom*' pain, that's what it is. I knew you wouldn't know that."

Blake's defeated eyes shift to the floor.

All the tension unsettles Sylvia. "I'm good," she lies as she winks at the quarrelsome father. "That talk doesn't rile me, Professor."

"Fine then," he says as his hook repositions the pipe hanging out of his mouth. He then looks at his watch. "Didn't you say that you have some fishing to do?"

Sylvia stands up and looks around, ignoring the rudeness of his question. She studies the shotguns and animal hides hanging from the log-paneled walls. "Yes, well, time does goes by, doesn't it?"

She notices that this cabin has electricity and is well lit and appointed, much better than *her* cabin, anyway. "I best go back to my place."

As Professor Barnes and his son Blake escort Sylvia to the door, she glances back at Silver-Wolf, whose eyes are still glued to the fire. The sheriff pays the departing visitors no attention whatsoever.

"Goodbye Silver-Wolf. Nice to have met you," offers Blythe.

The young Indian woman nods as she responds in her smooth, calm voice. "You'd best not pay any heed to Black-Tongue. No, no heed. What he says may be so, but may *not* be so . . ."

As she departs, Sylvia realizes that the warning is too late—she's already obsessed by Black-Tongue's words.

Furthermore, she's eager for his visit to the Crawler cabin.

* * *

The lake is choppy and as cold as Lucifer. Sylvia rows in the twelve-foot rowboat toward the point about a quarter-mile opposite Squaw Peak and two hundred yards from the Crawler cabin shoreline, reputed to be the deepest water in Lake Tahoe. To her, the water there looks no different than in the rest of the lake, except perhaps, she wonders, maybe a bit more turbulent.

The small portable radio—her only sop to electronic media—blares out a scratchy tune of country music as she looks up at the gathering, dark clouds. The wind's up too. Despite her heavy, red Parka, woolen pants and mittens, and brown, imitation-fur ski cap, the cold bites harder and harder, the temperature dropping fast.

Having thrown anchor with no bottom, she pulls up on her fishing line as she patiently sits starboard on the narrow bench, near the stern. So far, there's not even so much as a nibble on the hook.

Presently, the sun sinks behind the peak. Darkness engulfs her. Having forgotten her lantern, she's thankful that the moon is near full.

The shimmer of the dark blue water in the moonlight is mesmerizing, reminding her of a huge cauldron of boiling, churning tar. She'll give it a few more minutes, and then will call it quits. The news comes on the radio, and she reaches down beside her and turns up the volume . . .

"Strange weather for this Thanksgiving weekend. The severe snowstorm—so unusual before December—may hit the Tahoe area sooner than expected. Our dangerous weather advisory starts Saturday—*tomorrow*—the twenty-fifth—instead of Monday."

Sylvia turns the volume up even higher.

"However, our chief meteorologist calculates that the *brunt* of the storm should still hit Monday, when temperatures expect to fall to record levels. Furthermore, Saturday is the same day as the full lunar eclipse, not seen since eighteen sixty-seven. Due to the inclement weather you may not actually see it if you look for it outdoors tomorrow evening. Quite a coincidence . . . "

Sylvia turns off the radio, mulling over this unwelcome news. Part of her commands that she get out of there now and take the kids home. However, a strong urge to stay until Sunday, as planned, then takes hold. She feels that something needs to play out. Her destiny begs affirmation. Her curiosity demands satisfaction. Besides, the storm probably won't hit hard until Monday . . . "

Just then, the fishing line almost jerks her into the water.

A whopping force resists her as she struggles to reel in her prey. A huge fish is tugging at her line!

The pole and the line are strong, Sylvia figures, and they'll hold. She decides to try to reel in the catch. Repeated, forceful tugs, hoping to counteract the force of the fish and the strong current, produce little progress.

She jumps up from her seat, planting her leg sideways to support the powerful arching of her back. She thrusts her torso, fighting the pull on the line. Her fears of being jerked overboard into the ice cold water consume her. She inadvertently knocks the radio into the lake, it disappearing quickly below the whitecaps.

Sylvia's finally making headway, and sees that the catch is now just below the water's surface. She yanks the line, arching backward again and again, reeling in more. She sees the large object at the end . . .

Sylvia is as still as a statue, frozen in horror.

She doesn't even feel her heavy breathing. Her heart races as she rejects what she sees with her own eyes. What she retrieved from the freezing depths is not a big fish, but a body. Moreover, the corpse appears to be a woman!

Sylvia surmises that the intense cold—plus the lack of predators at that extreme depth—has preserved this poor victim. Sylvia slowly brings her in, observing the bluish tint of the nude body. As she pulls, she finds—to her amazement—that the woman looks familiar.

The body being too heavy to lift into the boat, Sylvia positions it along side. There appears to be no sign of life—the eyes being closed and no movement in the limbs. She grabs her coil of rope and ties it around the corpse's torso under the armpits, then ties the other end to the railing. She'll row back to the cabin, about two hundred yards off—if she *can*. She's getting weak, and, having gotten wet, is chilled in the powerful wind.

While fumbling with the knot near the body's neck, she gets a closer look at the hapless young woman's face. Terror stabs into Sylvia's gut as her breath leaves her.

The strange woman looks like—*her*!

The wide mouth is agape, showing the edge of her teeth. Sylvia can make out the gleam of the gold incisor on the bottom row of the squared jaw. She scans the corpse. The height looks similar. The hair color is identical and the freckled nose matches too. Even the breasts look the same!

Then she studies the body's left shoulder. *There's no tattoo. Thank God!*

Sylvia leans over the boat, her head very close to the blond head of the body. She rips off her mitten, forcing the left eyelid open with her freezing fingers.

Sylvia cups her mouth in horror at what she's discovered. Her tongue turns to cotton. She clearly sees the rare birthmark—a black dot at the border of the left, blue iris, at the three o'clock position.

It's just like *hers*!

Although not everything matches, she now fully realizes the significance of what she found.

That *thing* in the water is—*me!*

Or, is it the well-preserved body of the Wagon Master's wife, the Sylvia Crawler of long ago, as she existed on that horrible night in eighteen-sixty seven?

Part Two

As Sylvia frantically rows to shore, the sky fills with black clouds and the wind is ever more powerful—the whitecaps grow huge. The temperature drops drastically. Out of breath, her back and arms burn from the strain of rowing. Her breathing is labored. She curses the extra drag from the body tied to the rowboat. Waves splash over the side of the vessel, filling the bottom with water.

Then, hail, as big as gulf balls, catapult from the sky, some hitting her on the head and shoulders, the sting crippling. She notices the puffs of white air shooting from her mouth as her warm breath meets the freezing night. A thick fog is rolling onto the shoreline, complicating her navigation.

A massive whitecap hits on the port side, deluging the boat with freezing water. Another pounds her boat. The interior is filled. A third hits, and the boat capsizes about fifty yards off shore. Sylvia is thrown into the frigid lake.

The ice-cold water is like a thousand wasps stinging her at the same time, all over her body. She fights to keep her head above the surface. She glances at where the boat used to be, now gone, with the body gone too.

Her strength is dissipating. Never a good swimmer, she strokes as hard as she can and kicks her legs—the numbness ensuring that she cannot feel her feet. She is closer to shore, now just about twenty yards. She can see the dock.

Presently, the white caps are even bigger, pillaring the beach. She makes slow progress to the safety of land . . .

Sylvia staggers along the shore, fighting her way to the cabin in the horrendous sleet and wind. Her mind is almost gone, her numb body almost frozen. She thinks of the nude body in the lake. She feels that she is nude also, maybe stripped of sanity and hope. Then, she sees her cabin directly ahead. She notices the yellow horse hitched to the porch rail.

There must be a visitor.

* * *

The Crawler kids, joined by the arrival of Black-Tongue at their cabin just an hour before Sylvia staggered through the front door, freezing—draped in a tarpaulin that had covered part of the woodshed—sit in a circle around the roaring fireplace with their distraught mother. The shooting flames animate their dour expressions, and the flickering light twists their features.

The rest of the Crawler cabin is dark, except for a few lanterns strewn about the cabin. The nearly full moon is shining through the window, its hue slightly bluish. Sylvia wears a thick robe and slippers. She is still shaking from the biting cold and her ordeal on the lake. The others—besides Black-Tongue—wear jeans and a variety of pullovers, except little Adam, who is garbed in his woolen pajamas and moccasins. Black-Tongue had brought the moccasins for him as a special gift.

The Medicine Man reclines in a leather easy chair very close to the fire, peering out the window at the moon. He wears his tribal buckskin shirt and buffalo-leather trousers. A huge necklace made of eagle bones strung together with palomino mane hangs from his wrinkled neck. Black and white eagle feathers hang from the bones.

Yellow horses are coveted by the tribe, and are reserved for its leaders. Black-Tongue is renowned for his tribal jewelry made of the revered eagle and the hairs of the honored horse. Some say that these ornaments protect from evil spirits, some say the opposite. The old man draws the heavy Indian blanket up from his moccasins and drapes his knees and thighs with it, its extra warmth causing him to smile.

His eyes shift to his hosts gathered around the hearth. "An old man's bones are like the bones of an eagle—hollow. Warmth from fire is good. The night is like ice."

His smile widens more, revealing just two yellow teeth. "I shall let the fire die down, so we may talk to it."

The kids look at each other, exchanging knowing glances, as if telling each other: "Boy, is this old guy nuts."

Sylvia sits silently—her face blank—seemingly drained and pale by the terrible ordeal she has just survived. She didn't mention a word of this to her kids or to Black-Tongue. She didn't want to get too familiar with that old man.

Sylvia sips on a small glass of Cognac, her face a mask of impassivity. "What do you mean, Black-Tongue? You're scaring my children. They know that you can't talk to a fire." She slams her glass down on the armrest. "The weather is getting worse. You ought to leave soon, or the trail will be buried in ice and snow."

"I'm OK, Mom," insists Ben. "We're all good. I want to see the fire talk to Black-Tongue."

Adam jumps down from his chair and goes to his mother's lap, crawling on top. "Black-Tongue is nice, Mommy."

Blythe glances at daughter Sylvia. They both fold their arms and roll their eyes.

"All right. You two don't need to have an attitude," snaps Ben, glaring at his sisters. "If you don't want to hear it, just go up to bed. Don't spoil the fun."

Blythe sticks her tongue out at her brave brother, and Sylvia junior scowls. The fire is weaker.

Sylvia pats little Adam on his shaggy head. "You shall go back to your chair now, like a good boy."

Adam waddles back to his seat, as mother Sylvia's eyes narrow on the old man. She tightens her lips. She feels a twitch in her cheek.

Black-Tongue stands over the hearth as he places his hand into the flames. He holds it there for five seconds, without making a sound. He then removes it. He takes his blanket and smothers the fire with it.

Smoke escapes from its edges. As he lifts the blanket, the smoke billows up in large clouds of lavender soot, forming odd shapes and patterns that glow. Black-Tongue repeats the process three times. Each time he removes the blanket the shapes assume more defined forms.

His shrill, atonal voice fills the room. "Tree-people. Tree-people that glow. The full moon will be here. Then *not* here."

Sylvia's eyes are transfixed—and so are the kids'.

Black-Tongue raises his hands palms up over his head, his eyes shut. "Tree-people rise slowly," he continues, "they are slow, like an old woman. In the end, they do what they must. The new night will belong to the evil moon."

The old man then raises the blanket off the fire a fourth time, and this time the smoky billows assume the shapes of people floating over the fireplace, rising higher and higher to the ceiling, then dissipating. One small shape appears to be a little girl. The smoky apparition next to it appears to be a woman. The woman merges into the girl, and then forms one purple cloud. The little girl and woman are one—then gone.

"Stop it!" shouts mother Sylvia. "You're crazy, Black-Tongue!"

Ben pops to his feet. "No, let him finish! This is great. How does he make the smoke look like that? It's magic."

"Shut up, Ben," snarls daughter Sylvia. "You heard mother. Let's all go to bed. This is nothing. It's not much different than blowing smoke rings with a cigarette."

Ben is silent, his mouth wide open in amazement as Blythe—who covers her face with her hands—shouts: "I don't want to see any more." She dashes from her chair to the stairwell, tearing up the steps to the refuge of her bedroom. Sylvia junior and Adam follow her.

"You go with them, Ben," commands his mother. "Right now. Look after them."

Ben shakes his head. "But Momma—"

"I said—*get!*"

Ben obeys, following his siblings to the bedrooms upstairs.

Black-Tongue, oblivious to all this fussing, removes his charred blanket from the fireplace and hobbles over to Sylvia. He drapes the blackened and smoking blanket over his stooped shoulders.

"I must give you something before I go."

The old man digs into his pocket and removes his decoration, presenting the tribal bobble to Sylvia. His intense eyes burn into hers. "Here; it may help you."

Sylvia takes the object in her hands. She sees the flat, oval decoration with a small white circle on a dark background. It still has the same musty smell. He offered her the same ornament in the clinic. This time, she puts it in her robe pocket, to later hide under her bed.

"That is thoughtful of you Black-Tongue. Now, you must go."

"I must speak," he says in a whispering voice. "The tree-people—the people that glow. You saw a woman and little girl become one."

"Yes," agrees Sylvia. "I saw."

Black-Tongue clears his throat. His scratchy, weak voice continues. "The white woman Crawler—long ago with the wagons. On that night of ice and hunger . . ."

The Medicine Man's eyes narrow, forming slits. His speech is halting. He studies Sylvia for a moment and then falls silent, as if the epiphany had struck him dumb. "I must go." He starts for the door, seemingly eager to get on his horse and ride away. She follows him.

The brunt of the freak snowstorm may very well come early, mulls Sylvia as she walks to the door with her visitor. *It will come with the disappearing moon—just like a hundred and fifty years ago.* She can hear the wind getting stronger, now with heavy snow—not sleet—hitting the window. The cold bites harder—even inside with the fire.

Before she closes the door behind the departing Black-Tongue, his searching eyes find hers. Sylvia's stares at him, almost absently. "OK Black-Tongue. What else must you tell me?"

The Medicine Man's lips part in what could've been taken for a tight smile—more of wonder than mirth. "The Shoanah had evil in their hearts that night long ago," he explains. "On that night of the dying moon—the white woman Crawler ate all her children, but one."

* * *

Sylvia hears pounding on her bedroom door, which wakes her up from a deeper slumber than she can remember having since she had been a child. She opens her eyes, the crusts of sleep almost gluing her lids shut. She glances out the window, and although there's morning light, most of the window is white with piled snow.

The pounding at the door is louder. "Come on in. It's not locked," she hollers in a scratchy voice.

Ben strides into the room. He's dressed in full snow kit. "Sorry Mom, but the storm hit hard last night. Everything's buried in snow. The car too! I cleared the front porch and door with the shovel the best I can."

Sylvia, wearing her silk pajamas, climbs out of bed and throws on her robe. Black-Tongue's ornament falls out of the pocket and onto the floor. She picks it up and stuffs it under the mattress.

"What's that?" Ben asks.

"Nothing," she answers, "just a trinket that Black-Tongue gave me—sort of a good luck charm." Sylvia races over to the window, peering out of it. "My goodness, it's piled up to the second floor, and then some."

"The front of the cabin's a little better," adds Ben.

Sylvia frowns. "Think I can get into the car?"

"No. Bad news, Mom. The car isn't just buried. The winds must've been real bad, 'cause a huge pine's fallen on the Forrester. Another looks like it may fall any time. The trees are top-heavy with ice."

She steps into her slippers. "Let's go look."

Ben stares at his mother, his expression grave. "Feel OK Mom? You look pale. You move a little stiff and slow, too. What happened out there on the lake?"

"Oh, I don't remember much, except the boat capsized and I swam to shore."

Sylvia peers into the mirror above the little dresser. She sees that her eyes are bloodshot and there's a pink rim around her lips. Her complexion is chalky. "I'm all right. Just tired, that's all." She quickly changes the subject. "You stay away from that car! It's dangerous. Let's go downstairs and have a look around."

"You'd best dress real warm," coaches Ben, "it's mighty colder than yesterday. I'll bet the *big* storm hits *today*. The clouds are bigger and blacker. The wind's acting up, too."

"How are the kid's doing?" asks the mother.

"Sleeping; they're fine."

Sylvia throws off her robe and slippers, and then goes to the closet. She dons her heavy clothing over her pajamas: a Parka with a ski-sweater underneath, mittens, woolen slacks, snow-boots, and a fur hat. She and Ben head for the door.

"Something I haven't told you, Mom. There's some strange stuff outside, just below the awning. I found it partially buried this morning—dug it out—"

"What kind of stuff?"

"You'd best look yourself."

"You go down. I'll be with you directly."

Sylvia stumbles into the bathroom and sees that she tripped over an elevated plank of maple in the flooring. "Must be rotted," she comments to herself. Then, she notices a thin space between the planks. She kneels down and jams her finger into the crack. The plank elevates, revealing a small compartment.

"My lord—what do we have here?"

Sylvia lifts a small cigarette case from under the floor. She holds it up to the light coming through the small window. It looks to be gold—but oxidized and tarnished. She wedges open the case and sees a small photograph. It's a faded, close-shot of a middle aged woman.

This looks like Sylvia Crawler, she notices.

She flips it over and mumbles the inscription, probably—from the ornateness of the font—written by Sylvia herself: "Sylvia, loving wife of Wagon Master Josiah Crawler, eighteen-sixty-six."

The image includes a tight view of her face, and, although grainy, the left eye is clearly visible. Sylvia can barely see the dot near the left iris—in the same position as hers. She also notes that the style of the handwriting is very similar to hers. With a neutral expression, she defiantly rips the photo into tiny pieces, and then throws them in the toilet.

"There," she says as she flushes. "That takes care of that. The kids can't find it now."

* * *

Ben and Sylvia stand over a pile of debris just to the left of the front porch railing, where the trail that leads to the tribe used to be before it was buried in snow.

The mother had confirmed that the car situation is hopeless, and with it the phones and laptops—not that they necessarily would've worked anyway in the mountains and inclement weather. They leave the front porch and hike through the deep snow to get a better look at what Ben had found, wallowing in knee-high snowdrifts. In some places, it had piled up much higher than others.

Presently, they stand at the spot, looking down at the mess of snow—stained with red— that lay on the ground. The appalling sight forces Ben two steps back. He turns his head, losing his breakfast, and then returns to his mother's side, wiping his mouth with his coat-sleeve. He averts his eyes. "I told you it looked bad."

Sylvia's eyes remain fastened on the horror that popped out from under the very light snow that's falling around them. The fresh snowflakes are tinged with yet more blood—tinting some the area a gruesome pink. She picked up a small tree branch, brushing the ice off the grim findings, moving the pieces of skin and bones around— lying next to what is left of someone's clothing.

Sylvia considers the femur bone to be human—not animal. The predators of the forest seem to have had quite a feast. Some of the bones, however, are *not* human. Humans do not have hoofs. Then, she sees the long, narrow, fleshy skull with the rows of sturdy molars set in the narrow jaw. The eyeballs have been eaten away.

"When did you find this Ben?"

"About three hours ago," Ben's head is still slightly turned away, but he sneaks a peek here and there, "when I checked on the girls."

Sylvia pokes at the snow—uncovering more grisly articles.

That's when she sees the patch of yellow horse skin. Next, a piece of a buckskin shirt appears, and then part of the buffalo-leather trousers. Black and white eagle feathers hang from some smaller bones.

"What's that, Mom?"

She sighs, shaking her head. Her voice is soft. "That's—the remains of Black-Tongue and his palomino horse. That long skull is a horse's skull."

"What happened to them?" asks Ben in a strained voice.

"Must've been caught in the storm, son. Then the animals got to them."

Ben looks at the remains again, this time with more fortitude. "What's that?"

He points to a spot about three feet away from the piece of the Medicine Man's shirt. "Right there. That long thing with—a black tail."

Sylvia digs at it with her stick, unearthing more. "Go back inside Ben, tend to the girls. Then come back here and bury the remains. I don't want little Adam or Blythe to see this."

"What is it?" the son insists.

Sylvia lets out a deep breath. "Looks to me like the hindquarter of a horse, stripped of its skin." The mound of half-eaten flesh of the horse's behind sticks out of the snow. "That palomino had a lot of meat on him," she mutters under her breath. "I said, go inside Ben!"

Ben does as he's told. Sylvia looks over the remains of the hindquarter very carefully. She bends over it, studying the teeth marks on the remaining flesh.

The teeth marks do not look like they're from an animal.

They rather look *human*.

Ben returns with Blythe and Adam in tow. They stand on the porch. Sylvia glances their direction, looking up at her kids above her. She sees that daughter Sylvia is not with them. Ben's eyes betray that he's mighty worried, and that's not like him, she frets.

"Where's Sylvia?" screams the mother.

"Mamma," shouts Ben. "I checked everywhere. She's gone!"

* * *

Sylvia and Ben search every square inch of their cabin for the oldest daughter, and then scour the perimeter of the property. They find nothing—not even footprints. That isn't surprising considering the snowfall.

Ben almost collapses into a huge snowdrift at the rear of the property. His mother has to pull him out. They hike around the cabin one last time, and then end up at the porch, empty-handed. The sun—what can be seen of it—is straight overhead, indicating that it's nearly noontime.

"I'm going to Sylvia's room and search around. There might be something in there that will clue us in on where she went. Then, I'm hiking over to the Barnes' cabin."

"I'll go with you--"

"No Ben, you stay here!" Sylvia places her mitten firmly on her son's muscular shoulder. "Mind the kids."

Ben nods. He looks up at the sky. "Look at those clouds, Mom; never seen a sky so black. The wind's powerful too—"

Sylvia, observing the gathering storm, zips the hood of her Parka over her fur cap. "Temperature's dropping—quite a bit. Rustle up some lunch for Adam and Blythe while I go upstairs. I'd best get a move on if I'm going to slog over to the neighbor's cabin."

"Mom," Ben pleads. "Stay here. *I'll* go. You don't look so good. You look pale and tired—not like you."

"I've got a flu coming on. No big deal. You just stay here—you understand me?"

"Yes ma'am."

Sylvia walks up the staircase to her daughter's bedroom, running into her kids. She sees they're still in their woolen pajamas. "You two get some clothes on. Dress warm. There's a big storm coming." She passes them. "After lunch, help Ben carry the firewood from the shed. I'll be gone for a short while. Put a lantern in the shed, we may need it."

Sylvia reaches her missing daughter's room and closes the door behind her, locking it. She finds nothing in the small dresser and nothing suspicious with the floorboards. No secret passage out of the cabin is found, and no sign that the small window—frozen shut—had been tampered with. The snowdrifts next to the window would hamper anyone entering or leaving.

Sylvia has saved the closet for last. She scours every nook and cranny—finding nothing to help in her search. As she shuffles through some dirty clothing, she sees her daughter's small leather purse.

She opens the purse. She removes the beaded object—the same flat, oval decoration that Black-Tongue had given her. The small white circle on a dark background is unmistakable. It still has a musty smell. It's probably the same one, she figures.

Sylvia wonders: *How did she find it under the bed?*

Sylvia stuffs the bobble deep into the pocket of her Parka, and then heads to the front door. She decides to hike to the Indian village first, where Black-Tongue lived. Then, if her daughter's not there, on her return she'll detour back by the Barnes' cabin to look for her there.

* * *

All of a sudden, the sky breaks loose with a torrent of rain and sleet—that quickly turns to thick snow flurries. The wind howls as Sylvia slogs around near the cabin, barely plowing her way through the mounting snowdrifts. It's afternoon, but the sky's almost as black as midnight.

The full moon will be out in a few hours, she figures, and soon there'll be the total eclipse. Then, the darkness will be almost absolute.

As Sylvia wanders about trying desperately, lantern in hand, to find the trail to Indian Village, she realizes that it'll be impossible to see under the thick snowfall. She staggers over near the porch and sees that the beginning of the trail to the Barnes' place is still visible.

She stumbles onto the trail, her legs sinking to her knees. She can generally tell, however, where the trail goes due to the line of absent trees along the path's clearing in the thick forest. As she hikes, less and less of the tree-trunks are visible—the depth of the snow increasing. Nevertheless, the path between the treetops can be spotted through the thick of the blizzard.

Finally, after an hour of churning her weary, nearly frozen legs, she sees the top of the Barnes' cabin about thirty yards off. As she gets closer, the structure looks to be almost buried in snow.

What's left of the window is iced over, and no smoke comes from the primitive chimney—not a good sign. The temperature has dropped to well below zero, as white puffs of heavy breath shoot from her mouth. She sees the top half of the front door and she digs out the rest of it, her hands freezing-cold under her mittens.

She strains, jerking the door open with one hand while she holds her lantern in the other, just wide enough to squeeze through. To her surprise, one lantern still burns inside. The electric lines must've been knocked out by the freak storm hours before.

Sylvia ambles through the main part of the seemingly deserted cabin, and sees the hearth—still with a trace of glow in the cinders. At least, someone's been there recently, she surmises. Her breath is just as visible as outside—it being almost as cold inside the cabin.

There's no sign of Professor Barnes, his son, and most importantly—her daughter Sylvia. Just as she is about to search the rest of the cabin, she notices what looks like a flesh-colored blanket hanging behind the fireplace, on the far wall.

She approaches it very slowly, holding the lantern up to the curious discovery. She stands close to it, finally realizing what she's staring at. She inches forward to get a closer look.

Hanging from a peg on the wall is Professor Barnes—or rather— just his skin and some bones: his innards having been scooped out of him like an over-ripe avocado.

The strands of red hair still attach to the scalp atop his fleshed skull, and his horn-rimmed eyeglasses rest on the wooden floor, unbroken and clean. What's most pathetic is that his prosthetic arm and hook are still attached to the hollowed-out left arm, from just below the bone of the elbow.

Sylvia then backs up and quickly searches the rest of the cabin, with no trace of anyone else—alive or dead. At least her daughter is away from this place, and maybe safe and sound, she figures. Maybe she's back at the cabin, already having found her way home?

Nearly sundown, Sylvia decides to make her way back as soon as possible, while she can make it back at all. The snowstorm is bound to get worse—fast. Ben and the others must be frightened. They must be desperately waiting for her.

* * *

The snow piles higher as Sylvia slogs her way back to her cabin, holding the lantern high over her head. It's nighttime, but—despite the cloud-cover and snowfall—the full moon breaks through a small clearing, shining down on her like a lavender beacon.

As her hands and nose freeze, and her legs turn to rubber, she observes the increasing fog and mist rolling in—tinted purplish by the moon. As she fights her way back, her thoughts turn not so much to her plight, but to the ordeal of the Crawler Party, when the original Sylvia Crawler and her family fought for their lives. It's as though that incident has taken over her senses, an obsession that inserts into her consciousness automatically.

Suddenly, she notices that the purplish mist—and indeed the forest and snow around her—seem dimmer, less vibrant. She looks up at the sky as she churns her legs frantically through the deep snow to get back home.

The moon slowly disappears to pitch black. The light from a few twinkling stars that escape the snowstorm's canopy allow her to see at least partially. It's finally here, she marvels: *the full lunar eclipse!*

As if it's a reflex action, Sylvia dips her hand into her jacket pocket and pulls out Black-Tongue's beaded ornament—the white circle on the oval, dark background. She feels a surge of lethargy—and—a strange elation. She tucks it back in her pocket.

Bone-tired, aching, and hungry, she feels those bodily sensations slowly draining from her. A numbing determination takes over. She feels different somehow: less alive but better equipped to handle the rigors at hand. She had read that this is the way of survivalists facing lethal conditions outdoors.

Sylvia spots her cabin—the light of the window shining through the thick snowfall just a bit away. Smoke comes from the chimney. The temperature plummets to finger-numbing levels. The lantern gives out. She throws it away as she approaches the front porch.

Just then, she sees for the first time the fleeting, glowing figures amongst the silhouettes of the trees. They have a purplish caste, just like the moon had. They seem, to her, as very distant relatives. There are hundreds of them. She can even make out that some wear cowboy hats and bonnets. Some miss body parts. They make a grunting—and whining—sound.

My God, it's them! The tree-people are here—like the figures that rose from Black-Tongue's blanket at the fireplace.

Then again, she's not that surprised to see them at last . . .

The apparitions approach her—with their arms outstretched. She just makes it to the door. The figures are ravenous and freezing—desperate! Plowing through the snow, and just in time before one of the freaks catches up to her, she bangs hard on the front door and it opens wide.

* * *

"Mom, Sylvia got here about an hour before you did."

Ben sits beside the fireplace, warming his hands, as Blythe and Adam—their eyes wild with fear—hang on to their big brother's every word. Ben glances from his mother over to daughter Sylvia. "We heard her pounding on the front door. She hasn't said a word since she's been here. I don't know why she disappeared."

"Darling. Are you OK?" She ignores her mother's question and sits perfectly motionless, except for her blinking eyelids. Sylvia, sitting next to her, strokes her daughter's hair—still matted and damp from the harsh outdoors. She looks very pale. The windows thud with snow and hale; the wind howls. "What happened to you out there, dear? Why did you disappear?"

She just sits there, nodding absently, saying nothing. She's sickly and lethargic, staring into the fire. Her wet Parka lies on the floor but she still wears her damp woolen slacks, shirt, and hiking boots. The rest of the kids wear their warm Parkas, jeans, and sneakers, including little Adam, who is silent and sullen.

Sylvia studies her daughter closely and shakes her head. "Something happened to her out there—something bad. She's in shock."

The mother smiles reassuringly to Adam and Blythe. "Your sister's a little ill, that's all. It's quite a storm out there. It may get worse, too. I think the brunt of the freak snowstorm they expected is arriving *now*—not tomorrow as originally expected." Sylvia's eyes then meet Ben's. "We'll be all right. We must pull together—"

Ben's hands shake. "Mom, did you see those—*things*—out there, wandering around in the trees?" He glances out the window, as if expecting one to wave through the glass. "Not *people*—don't know what. They glow like fireflies—only a funny color."

"I need to get sister out of these wet clothes." Sylvia ignores her son's question, as though not discussing it will make the unpleasant facts go away. "I'll take her upstairs and get her into a warm bath and pajamas."

She stands up from the chair and then helps her daughter up too. "The temperature's dropped something fierce. You all better make sure you're wearing your long underwear." She places her hand gently under Sylvia's elbow and leads her to the staircase.

"Mom, you OK?" asks Ben in a nervous tone.

"Yes, Ben—I'm all right. Worried, that's all; tired and sick, too. Phones are out; car's buried. Neighbors are . . . " Sylvia pauses when considering the fate of Professor Barnes and his missing son. Best not go there, she decides. "The trails have disappeared in the storm."

Sylvia climbs the staircase with her daughter at her side. Out of the corner of her eye, she sees Ben placing his CD player near the fireplace. She glimpses her kids sitting near the flames, their faces lit up like jack-o'-lanterns.

Sylvia's teenage daughter moves with fluid, deliberate steps at her side, like slow motion. The spiral staircase creaks. "By morning, the snowstorm should break—then maybe we can get outta here," she gently reassures Sylvia.

Presently, the women are in the upstairs bathroom, and the mother is drawing the hot bath. Surprisingly, there's still warm water and pressure in the plumbing—but probably not for long. She peels the wet clothing from her daughter's body and helps her into the tub. Picking up the washcloth next to the stack of dry clothing on the chair, she wets it with the bathwater and then lathers it with a soap-bar. Daughter Sylvia stands in the tub with her smooth back facing her mother, her head just below the small, steamed window.

Sylvia washes her daughter as she stares at the window, which looks to be half-covered in snow. The wind has grown louder. "Sit down in the tub honey, so I can lather your lovely golden hair. Careful."

She remembers that the snowdrifts are piled higher at the rear of the property. Her mind, however, is curiously devoid of fear and dread, considering the circumstances. She starts to hum a tune that just comes to her—a western folk melody that she hasn't sung since she was a kid: *She'll Be Comin' Round the Mountain*.

"Get up from the tub, dear," says Sylvia. "I'll dry you. Step into these nice thick pajamas here."

As her daughter steps down onto the wooden floor, the mother's eyes fix on her daughter's left shoulder. She sees a tattoo: a white circle on an oval, dark blue background. The mother studies it with no reaction. She had never seen the tattoo on her before, but she hasn't had occasion to in quite a long time, either.

Her daughter dresses herself with her assistance. As she puts on her top, she whispers in a soft voice. "Thank you, Mama."

Sylvia is relieved by the communication.

"You'll be fine, dear."

Glass shatters—then an arctic blast hits Sylvia in the face.

Snow and wind are sucked into the room as she swerves around, toward the smashed window. A man's icy arm shoots through it—the hand large and blue—with bloody nails. The sleeve above it is full of maggots. The hairy hand sweeps in powerful, rapid arcs, the fingers forced into claws—opening and closing—trying to hook Sylvia and her daughter, who cower just a few feet away.

Sylvia grabs her stunned daughter and dashes for the bathroom door, glancing back at the horrific intruder—its torso and head now visible. The unsightly thing squeezes the rest of the way through the window—just barely. Sylvia grabs the lantern on the wall next to her and throws the door open. She drops the lantern.

Just before she slams the door shut behind her, she catches an eyeful of the creature—now closer—slithering toward the door. Its sweet, musky odor is sickening. It looks like a chewed up, rotted corpse. Its arms and claws thrust toward the terrified women. The bearded, mask-like face is like grey, molten wax. The eyes are just white ovals, with no color—except for tiny, central, black spots. Bluish lips gape, revealing broken teeth tinged in pink. Bloodstains are deposited at the mouth's corners.

It wears a strange suit of clothes—torn and wet—with a string tie from another era. Emitting a bizarre, shrill whimper, eerie tones of desperation and lust are evident within its repellant sound. The wild man glows with a purplish aura in the dim light . . .

Daughter Sylvia, suddenly animated, slams the thick, oaken door shut behind them. Cowing in the hallway with her daughter, mother bolts it from the outside. As the pounding on the bathroom door gets louder and louder, they tear down the hallway and then the stairwell to the safety of the bottom floor.

At the base of the stairs, Ben stands there in stunned silence. The Beach Boys song "Don't Worry Baby" is playing in the background from Ben's CD player. "What wrong, Mom? You look—"

His mother grabs him by his shoulders, shaking him. "There's a monster loose in the house!"

Part Three

Ben groups the girls, Adam, and his distraught mother around the fireplace, and then feeds the flames with more kindling as the surreal beach music plays in the background. He looks at his elder sister wearing her thick pajamas, who still seems to be in shock. Ben had poked his head upstairs for a second—seeing and hearing nothing unusual—and then scurried back downstairs to rejoin his family.

He studies his mother's face. She sits with the others in the chairs arranged around the fireplace, their faces lit up and distorted by the flickering light. She seems to be in shock too. *No wonder she's imagining things*, he realizes.

He picks up a blanket and drapes it around his sister's shoulders. "The wood's nearly gone," announces Ben, "I best go to the woodshed; fetch more—"

"The evil moon is upon us!" utters his mother softly.

She retrieves from her coat pocket Black-Tongue's gift of the beaded ornament—the white moon on the dark, oval background—and places it gently on Ben's armrest. Ben picks it up and looks at it, then shrugs and places it in pants pocket.

Poor mother must be sick, frets Ben. She's usually so strong. She shouldn't have been out of the cabin so long, in the blizzard. *And what happened to them upstairs*, wonders Ben? *Mother won't say a word about it. And why, before, did sis disappear?*

"Mom," says Ben as he fetches the shotgun off the fireplace mantle, "we'll freeze without more wood." He glances over at the window. "Thought I saw someone outside, wandering in the snow, " he continues, sighting his rifle. " He looked angry. Best tote this gun—"

"Let them in," instructs the mother absently as she stares into the fire. "Might be folks stranded."

Ben stands next to her with the gun. He realizes that his mom is not herself. "What happened upstairs, Mama? Why won't you tell me?"

"Do you hear anything dear," asks Sylvia.

"No. Not a thing." Ben frowns. She must have a fever, he figures. She looks even paler—sweating too. *Maybe I can get her to a doctor soon.*

"Daughter and I must've been imagining that man . . ." Her voice drifts off into a faint whisper, as if she's totally drained. "Chilling night," she adds under her breath.

Ben strides over to the window with his shotgun, leaving the crossbow—with its arrows—resting on the mantle-piece. He wipes off the glass, peering out into the darkness. His warm breath ejects white puffs. "Wow, is it cold out there! Never been a night so cold! It's cold in here, too."

"There's a total lunar eclipse going on," explains Blythe. "She gets up and goes over to the window to join Ben, leaving little Adam staring into the fire, as silent as a tomb. " Good thing there's some starlight."

She looks out through the glass. "See that, Ben? There's people out there wandering in the snow; they're all lit up, too—hundreds of them. You were right. They look angry—"

Ben gets a better look. "Mama! She's right. Hundreds!"

"I saw folks that looked like that at the Barnes cabin—with mamma," offers Blythe. "They floated out of the fireplace!"

Ben figures that his little sister might be a bit loony too.

Mother Sylvia just sits motionless in her chair, glancing over at Ben and Blythe, and then Adam, her absent gaze prolonged, as if in a trance. "Yes, *angry*," she repeats. "That's what they are. The *tree-people*; they glow in the dark." She speaks in a slow, weak, breathy voice. "It's an Indian moon going on out there."

Adam looks at his mother—his face frozen with fright. "Will they hurt us, Mama?" She doesn't answer him.

"An Indian *what*?" Ben asks his mother.

She is silent.

"Those things walking around out there," Ben says as he's looking out the window, "there're making weird sounds—I can hear it all the way in here; eating twigs, branches, and bugs too. They must be real hungry. Look—they're glowing purple Mom, just like you say! "

Ben's mother just nods, but says nothing. Her eyes are fixed on the fire. Suddenly, Blythe grabs a lantern and a basket hanging on the wall and dashes out the front door— into the cold darkness. She screams back to Ben, "I'm getting the kindling for the fire!"

Ben runs to the door and screams back, "Come back here! Blythe—you get in here right now!"

"We need it," she shouts back, running toward the shed.

Ben staggers out on the porch, leaving the door open a crack, the hard sleet hitting him in the face, the gusts of wind nearly blowing him over. He can barely make out Blythe's figure, trudging through deep snow and struggling to get to the woodshed.

The tree-people grab her.

They fight to get pieces of their prey, clawing at her eyes and yanking her arms, battling to bring her down. A man, one of his arms missing and his face nearly eaten away, throws his other arm around her small waist as another creature—a woman with blood oozing from her mouth—chews at little sister's neck. Blythe's lantern drops in the snow next to the half-rotted woman, and the creature moves away from it quickly, as if it were the plague.

Ben notices that the loathsome figure seemed to avoid Blythe's lantern.

Another one of those things, with half a face, has bright red hair with streaks of green in it. "Blake," screams Blythe as she frantically fights to escape from the creatures, "Blake Barnes! Help me!"

Instead of helping her, Bens sees that this person—who his sister seems to know—struggles with the others to pull her to the snowy ground. Blythe just manages to break his hold on her, when the man with one arm grabs her by the hair. He yanks it out by the roots—with part of Blythe's scalp with it.

Blythe screams with pain. "Blake! *Please* . . ."

Blake moves past the other creature, lunging little sister again, and Blythe, breathing hard and bleeding from the neck and scalp, just manages to plow through the snow to reach the door of the woodshed.

Ben jerks his head from the window and glances at his mother. "Get over here. Those things are hurting Blythe!"

Sylvia's fitful stare shifts from the fire to her son. She tries to speak to Ben, but can't.

Ben shouts, "Adam, you lock the door behind me, you understand?" The music playing sticks on the same song over and over again, as Ben rushes to the door and throws it open, firmly shutting it behind him, the cold almost bringing him to his knees.

He makes a dash for the shed to try to rescue his little sister, but is stopped in his tracks on the porch by a wall of slithering tree-people. They stumble toward him with surprising speed. Off the side of the porch, he can barely see Blythe, struggling to jerk its frozen door open. More creatures rush after her in the deep snow, frantically attempting to claw her away from the door. They tear at her clothes and try to pull the rest of her hair out by the roots.

His brave sister beats the attackers away. She finally forces the door open. Ben, barely seeing in the dark, even at this range, sees that sis is inside the shed. Its small window throws off light, and it's clear to Ben that she has lit the lantern stored in the woodshed. Then, Ben sees flames flickering behind the glass. As the seconds pass, the glass gets brighter as the fire inside the shed progresses. Smoke then wafts from the door—then flames.

Ben's eyes widen with terror. Sis must've dropped the lantern in the woodshed, setting the whole structure ablaze. Despite this, she remains inside. Ben figures—with horror—she decided that it's better to face the fire than those freaks that are after her.

She's burning!

The monsters on the porch are now grabbing at Ben, who fights them off by using his shotgun as a club. There must be a dozen of them. He can smell their musty, old-rag odor, and it makes him sick. He sees their grey skin, with sickly blue lips and hands. They wear old cowboy clothes—the kind he sees in westerns at the cinema.

Their clawed hands ravage Ben, his coat now torn. One has him by his collar. Ben jerks his body back, breaking its grasp, and then he lets him have it in the face with point-blank buckshot. The rifle reverberates as the head explodes in a cloud of grey flesh. The thing staggers backward holding its face, but then recovers and comes at Ben again.

Ben retreats to the front door, and then blasts the creature again, this time removing a chunk from its side. It pauses its slither for a few seconds, and then continues toward him once more, whimpering and groaning.

Ben wrenches the front door open. He dashes inside and bolts the thick door shut behind him. Wiping the sweat from his forehead, he realizes that he barely made it back into the cabin. Almost out of breath, He runs over to the window to see what's happened to Blythe . . .

The shed has disappeared into an orange ball of fire. Ben wipes the window and then observes a small figure—enshrouded in flames—shooting out of the shed and into the snow, rolling around in the cold substance in a frantic effort to smother the flames.

It's Blythe—she's fighting to stay alive!

Ben covers his eyes—his legs feel like rubber. In no time, the flames engulf his sister, and then die down, revealing a half-charred, doll-like figure resting in the snow—nearly motionless.

Ben glances over to the fireplace and his sister and mother, noticing that little Adam is gone. He shouts to his mother, "Where's Adam?"

They don't answer him. Ben rushes throughout the bottom floor of the cabin before he checks upstairs. He sees the CD players still stuck on his favorite song. Desperate and struggling, and half out of his mind he takes his rifle by the barrel and clubs the Sony player to pieces. The music's gone.

As he passes the window, he looks outside to see if Adam might have strayed out there before he was supposed to lock the front door. The fact is the door hadn't been locked when Ben dashed back into the cabin—not a good sign.

The horrific sight out the window nearly staggers Ben.

Blake Barnes plows through the snow to position himself at the blackened corpse of his little sister, violently pushing the other hungry creatures away from his catch. He reaches down, yanking pieces of Blythe's arm from her barbequed body—as if at a Hawaiian pig-bake. The rotted man with one arm joins the feast, and then the creatures start fighting over the morsels.

The things devour Blythe in huge gulps. Then, to Ben's utter horror, he witnesses Blythe's half-burnt body slowly rising, staggering through the snow to reach the front door of the cabin. The other creatures join her. On the way, she grabs at a little figure wandering pitilessly in the snow. She starts feasting on his little ear.

Ben realizes that it's Adam! *Blythe is eating little brother!*

Ben breaks the window with his rifle butt and fires his shotgun out the window. What's left of Blythe goes down. Adam makes a run for the porch, his little legs dropping into the snowdrifts so deep that only his head is visible above the snow. Somehow, Adam fights his way out of the snow and plows on toward the porch.

Ben decides that he will give Adam cover until he gets to the porch, then he'll make a dash out the door to meet him, whisking him back into the safety of the cabin.

Ben blasts away at Blake and he too goes down, and then slowly rises again from the snow. Other freaks are busy eating smoking pieces of Blythe's severed arm. Another zombie—an older woman in a blood-soaked bonnet, pulls Adam down into the snow. She pulls off his clothing as he fights with his little fists, and then the creature chews on his exposed neck.

Ben fires again twice, this time splattering not only Blake's torso, but also the head of the woman attacking his little brother. Both targets hit the snow. Within seconds, they are squirming and then getting to their feet again, trudging forward. Little Adam lay in the snow, bleeding from his neck—motionless and blue.

Ben—heaving with sobs—realizes that Adam and Blythe are gone and that there's nothing he can do about it.

With a ray of hope, he notices that the creatures are putting distance between themselves and the burning shed. This confirms that fire could be deadly to them.

He throws his rifle down, glancing over at the women. His sister and mother are in their own worlds. "Mama!" screams Ben. "Get a hold of yourself! Help me fight these things."

Sylvia just remains sitting quietly, stroking her daughter's thick hair. "Yes, they *glow*; tree-people," she whispers absently.

Ben hears loud pounding on the front door. He knows it's thick oak, bolted from the inside by the beam. It'll hold—at least for a while, he hopes.

He feels sick as he frets, again, over his little sister and brother's fate. He then loses his lunch, sticking his head out the broken window, to heave. Finished, he wipes his mouth, dropping to his knees. He starts to cry again.

Then, he slowly gets up and grits his teeth.

I'm going to fight! *I'm going to save my mother and my sister,* he resolves. They're too sick and weak to fight back. Fuck the creatures!

* * *

Now, there's more pounding on the front door. Ben rushes to it, and hears the sound of a girl begging him to open the door. The little girl's voice is familiar. Ben realizes it's Blythe—calling his name: *"Ben, Ben, I'm cold; please let me in."*

Ben unbolts the door, throwing it open. Blythe stands there, with a bloody knife in her hand, her skin bluish, her fiendish face like chalk, her dead eyes white ovals. She moves slowly toward her brother, most of her body a charred, putrid pulp, her half-chewed, remaining arm extended to him.

Ben picks up his shotgun, aims it, and blasts her in the face as the other freaks try to force their way into the cabin. Ben clubs them back with the rifle and bolts the door again.

He backs up. As he moves backward, he feels the impact of his body squishing against a solid object, reeking of rotted flesh.

He spins around with his gun and sees another little girl approaching, the white oval eyes and blue lips and hands indicating that she's one of the zombies. Ben glances over at the fireplace. It's flames dying; another creature is breaking into the cabin from the chimney, for he can see its dangling feet over the near extinguished flames. He realizes that's how the little girl got into the cabin. Ben blasts her point-blank, separating her little chest from the rest of her body.

Ben dashes over to the fireplace, blasting away at the dangling cowboy boots. He hears a kicking, whining sound as the boots make contact with the flames. He jams the rifle barrel up the chimney and blasts again for good measure. What's rest of the little creature—a young boy—plops into the fireplace, burning and smoking, the thing screaming a shrill, ear-splitting whine. Ben blasts him again, and then loads what's left of the kindling on the fire.

He hopes that the stronger fire will prevent more creatures from crawling down the chimney—at least for a while, since fire seems to be their enemy.

Just then, Ben hears glass shattering. The tree-people, grouped on the porch, are breaking into the cabin from what's left of the small window. It just might be big enough to let them squeeze through too, he figures.

Blood soaked arms and grey-blue heads are popping through the window. One small creature—it must be a child—is trying to come in legs and butt first.

Ben quickly reloads, and blasts the thing three times. It lets out an eerie whine and then lies motionless. It's now a pile of dry, grey mush, resting on the sill. But, there's enough left of his face for Ben to recognize. It's Adam—or what's left of him anyway! For a moment, Ben is so stunned that he can't move or think, and then gets a grip on himself, realizing it's do or die—not only for him, but the rest of the family as well.

He runs over to the box of shells over the fireplace and quickly reloads again, and shoves some cartridges into his pants pocket. After this, he realizes that he will be out of ammo.

He slings the gun over his shoulder by its strap, and tears over to the utility toolshed. He picks up the machete and hammer and stuffs them under his belt. He snatches some pieces of wood and some nails, and then dashes back to the window with his implements.

Pushing the Adam's grey goo from the sill and out to the porch, he nails slabs of wood over some of the window openings, blocking entry. He can feel the cold wind hitting his face as rotted arms and hands thrust toward him again through the few openings that remain.

A head—with a grey-hamburger face—pops through the window. Ben readies his shotgun and sites the creature, and then pulls the trigger, discharging his first shot into the horrific face.

Pieces of stale flesh spray Ben.

He leans his rifle against the wall, and then resumes boarding up the window. The window, however, is crammed with the flailing hands and arms of more tree-people. Ben retrieves his powerful automatic shotgun, and this time he lets go with four more blasts of his shotgun. He starts hammering again . . . but one of the monsters bashes the wood away.

Ben aims his shotgun, but when he pulls the trigger—there's only a click. Out of ammo, he throws down his gun and grabs his machete from under his belt. The monsters are pushing their meaty hands through the openings in the boards. One thrusts his arm deeper toward Ben, getting hold of Ben by his sleeve.

Ben whacks the arm with his machete, chopping it off clean. It falls into the cabin and plops on the wooden floor—bloodless. *The creepy things don't even bleed, he realizes!*

Another thing's fingers almost have Ben by his belt. He whacks through the fingers with the machete, like cutting weeds. He then chops wildly at the other body parts plugging the window, the creatures whimpering strangely as they retreat—for the moment anyway.

Another freak—a huge man with a worm-eaten head—sticks his face into the cabin from the window. Ben drops the machete, then grasps the hammer from under his belt—and bashes the creature's face—what is left of it anyway—until almost nothing is left of it. Ben drops the hammer and retrieves the machete.

He plops down on the easy chair, facing the window. The machete rests in his hand. He sits up and turns, catching his breath, glancing over at his mother and sister. They sit quietly at the fire, just as before.

Just then, he feels a powerful hand grasping his shoulder from behind. He can tell from the smell and strange grunts that it's one of the zombies. *It's loose in the cabin!*

Ben jumps up, breaking its grasp on him, spinning around with machete in hand, and chopping with all his might. He severs the head of the creature from its bloody, clothes-torn shoulders. The rest of the stinking flesh plops to the floor.

He can just make out the string tie as the torso crashes to the ground, lying motionless. Ben can see from the trail of bloody debris and mud-prints from its cowboy boots that it had just slithered down from the stairwell to his chair.

This is the thing, which attacked mother and sister while they were upstairs.

Ben goes over to the utility, laying the machete back behind the partition. He grabs more boards, then strides back to the window and finishes boarding it up. He moves over to the fireplace. Now the flames are bigger and the warmth more powerful, but he realizes it won't last long.

There's no more wood inside the cabin to burn. He hopes the fire will last until morning. The fireplace lights up his mother and sister's faces as his mother's eyes open wider, sensing the energy. She scoots her chair away from the flames. She looks at her son, shaking her head. "It's no use Ben."

A chill shoots down Ben's spine. *It can't be as hopeless as she says.*

His mother's voice is barely audible.

"The tree-people will win."

* * *

Ben—the Eagle Scout aspirant—diligently prepares for the new wave of the zombie attack. In some strange way, the shock of what's happened to him is wearing off, and he begins to appreciate the intense excitement of his task at hand—*survival.*

He takes the hoe and the hatchet from the utility and places it by the chairs next to the fire. He does the same with the crossbow perched on the mantle-piece above the fireplace, except the three arrows, which he crams under his belt. The gas and kerosene canisters have already been moved upstairs to the attic. He drags the sofa over to the window, stands it on its end, and nails the legs against the wall in order to block entrance.

Next, he moves the large easy chair against the front door to reinforce it, and then nails the bottom of the chair to the wooden floor planks—some if which are moldy and rotten.

Ben takes two of the largest meat carving knives from the kitchen area, and hands one to each his sister and his mother. Mother narrows her eyes, placing the weapon in her large coat pocket.

Ben dare not tell mother about little Adam and Blythe, fearing it might kill her. Sister Sylvia holds the knife and plays with it absently as she sits in her chair, seemingly oblivious to the dangers of their dire situation.

"Mom, could you make us something to eat? I saw plenty of cans in the kitchen." Ben nods toward his sister sitting quietly next to her. "I'll bet *she's* hungry too. These things seem to come in waves, so we may have a few minutes."

His mother gets up slowly from her chair and wanders over to the kitchen. She arranges the implements on the counter, preparing their dinner of cold beans on paper plates—with some tap water in plastic cups to wash it down with.

Meanwhile, Ben drags one of the chairs over to near the front door, plopping it down on the hard wooden floor. He lets out a huge sigh. He keenly observes the fire getting weaker, and prays that it lasts a few more hours. Looking at his watch, he sees that it's nearly midnight.

He had heard that the snowstorm is supposed to last about twenty-four hours, so by dawn it should pass—and the roads should be clear too. With it, there'll be help. He tries not to think about the freaks—*what* they are—*who* sent them here—and *why* they are . . .

Suddenly, there's heavy pounding on the front door. It gets louder as Ben rushes over to near the fireplace and grabs his crossbow. He hears the horrific whining. He grabs one arrow from under his belt and cocks and loads the bow. "Ma! They're back! You stay there. Sister will be OK by the fire."

Ben's mother is silent. Then, as if in a trance, she continues opening cans and arranging the plates and utensils for supper. The butcher knife hangs out of her coat pocket.

Ben glances over to the chairs next to the fire, but sister is no longer there. He glances back to the rear of the cabin, and sees that the oak door—leading to the makeshift outhouse attached to the cabin—is now closed. He figures she's using the latrine.

Pounding now starts to come from the window also. The sofa jolts with the force of the blows. A bluish hand shoots through a crack between the sofa and the boards nailed over the window. Ben dashes over and draws his bow, sighting his target.

A woman's head shoots through the opening, her gaping mouth toothless, with worms crawling out between her bluish lips. Her eyes—the blank white ovals—open and close almost rhythmically.

Ben lets go of an arrow. It hits just below her forehead, going straight though one of the hideous eyes. The thing emits an eerie grunt. Again, there's no blood. The head drops back into the darkness outside.

The front door—with the easy chair in front of it—crashes in with a tree trunk serving as a makeshift battering ram. Three creatures have the icy trunk in their clutches as they bash their way past the door, shedding chunks of ice and snow from their fetid garments. Ben shoots his second arrow and it pierces the throat of the first zombie, the creature—a man-like corpse—dropping to his knees. The arrow sticks out from the back of its neck.

The other two—young women in rotted and moldy dresses—drop the battering ram. They bat down the rest of the boards with their mangled hands. Ben shoots his last arrow, dropping the larger one as she grabs her chest.

The other one shuffles toward him. Other freaks that he had already killed or wounded rise from the ground and move toward him too, their white tongues hanging out, grunting, and whimpering. Ben glances over to his mother in the kitchen, who seems oblivious to everything—still in shock.

He quickly retreats to the flickering fireplace, grabbing hold of the hatchet leaning against a chair. The monsters slowly approach him, joined by scores of fresh ones that have just poured through the window and the door. Now, he sees that they are even entering through the chimney again. Ben can tell that the creatures are slowing, however, as they get closer to the fireplace—but the flames are dying for lack of fuel! He holds his hatchet ready . . .

He feels the planks under his feet moving. Two rotted planks in the floor pop up—then a dozen more—the wood breaking as it's being forced up from underneath. Ben figures that the freaks are infiltrating the crawlspace under the cabin.

Bluish, half-decomposed, mangled heads shoot up through the openings in the floor. Their putrid bodies climb into the cabin. Ben then feels something sharp crash into his upper back—the pain shooting to his neck. It almost brings him to his knees. He spins around to grab the creature—then lets out a scream . . .

It isn't a zombie—it's sister Sylvia at the non-business end of a hoe. Her face is not pale anymore but a deathly grey. Her eyes are white ovals. Her lips and hands are blue. She whimpers that guttural, desperate sound.

Ben lunges away from her, the hoe's blade tearing his flesh. He senses that the wound is probably superficial. He glances at his mother, who watches them with haunting detachment.

Ben realizes that his sister—sometime over the last several hours—had transformed into one of *them*. He pivots, swinging his hatchet wildly as he makes a powerful arc, the blade cutting solidly into his sister's neck. He swings again, severing her head as it thuds to the floor. She takes a few steps toward him, and then hits the floor—and stays there.

At first shocked by the horror of murdering his own sister, he realizes that that wasn't really his sister, but just something evil and non-human. He also realizes that these things *can* die, *or if not die, at least be slowed down.* He can't let things like remorse—for even chopping at his own sister and brother—fill his head. He must live. Besides, for some reason he can't understand, they had also transformed into one of *them*.

Ben looks around. Zombies surround him. He dashes to the fireplace, and sees the edge of a long piece of firewood that still has flames. He slides the hatchet handle under his belt. He snatches the torch out of the fire, burning his hand, and then dashes along the path to the kitchen that is not yet littered with creatures.

He grabs his mother's hand and pulls her with him, as he rushes up the staircase to the second floor, swinging his torch wildly to keep the freaks at bay. After a few steps, he sees a huge creature blocking the stairs. Ben sticks the torch in its face, setting it on fire.

Holding its burning face, the creature crashes down the stairs to the ground floor, almost taking Ben with him.

Ben pulls his mom along the hallway as more creatures chase after them, flooding onto the second floor. He sees the door to the attic at the end of the hall, and tears in that direction, his poor mother in tow.

She stumbles. Ben helps her to her feet. He grabs her hand again and thrusts toward the attic door, with the zombies close behind.

Finally reaching attic door, with his mother beside him, he feels the slimy hand of one of the creatures grabbing him by his shoulder. He shoves his torch into the meaty arm and the thing retreats. He pushes Sylvia into the attic before he leaps inside, bolting the thick door behind them.

Ben throws down the torch, and stomps it out. He removes the hatchet from his belt as his mother takes a seat on the chair, and he on the floor. They stare at each other, breathing heavily.

Sweat runs down from Ben's forehead as his hatchet rests on the floor next to him. It is dark inside, but enough lantern-light filters beneath the door to allow him to see the lantern hanging from the wall inside—the one poor sis had put there.

Ben takes the matches off the lantern and lights it. He stuffs the matches in his coat pocket, noticing the canisters of kerosene and gasoline resting upon the dusty shelf. Although dim inside, his vision is much better—especially after his eyes adjust to the darkness.

Suddenly, there's loud pounding and grunting at the door as the creatures try desperately to gain entry to the attic. The door is splintering. Ben figures that it will hold for a little while—how long, who knows? One thing for sure, there's too many of them to fight off this time.

He looks up at his mom. "You OK?"

"Yes, yes I'm fine, Ben."

"I *had t*o kill her, Mom. Sylvia's dead! Adam and Blythe too!"

"I know, Ben. Don't fret," she utters flatly. "You did your best, Ben."

* * *

The light of the huge bonfire reflects off the silver tooth of the rail-thin man with the salt and pepper ponytail. He chants atop a snowy hill overlooking Tahoe and the Crawler cabin. He's on his knees with a blanket that displays the Shoanah design—an oval, dark blue field with a small white circle in the middle—the sign of the Shoanah moon.

Throwing the blanket on the fire and almost smothering it, he then lifts it. Thick puffs of phosphorescent, purplish smoke fill the air, made more visible by the almost pitch-black sky of the full lunar eclipse.

He must work diligently, since the eclipse will be over very soon. The storm is already getting weaker and there's no more snowfall or even sleet. He lifts the blanket as he chants, and presently the smoke takes shape into human figures—white settlers billowing up, and then wandering desperately among the trees, with a few fallen innocents.

They make whining noises, beckoning their brethren from the depths of Tahoe to join them. Redfern's piercing gaze looks down onto the distant lake with no bottom—at its deepest point—from which purple apparitions rise into the black of night.

The apparitions hover over the whitecaps of the lake, herding onto the shore, slithering up among the pines to the Crawler cabin—fulfilling the curse of the Shoanah and commissioning the tribe's vengeance. It's revenge for the land stolen from their people generations ago—by nesters like Josiah Crawler. But for one, the Crawlers and their kin will parish—and not return to the earth.

It's tribal bad luck to wipe out a bloodline entirely, no matter what the offense.

Tom Redfern raises his hands palms-up in salute to the absent moon and the god of vengeance. He wears his tribal necklace over his wolf-furs and buffalo-hide trousers.

His headdress speaks of eagles flying high and bison roaming the range with their sharp horns. The blanket moves, the smoke rises, and the tree-people float up and savagely wander, just as the ones emerging from the bottomless lake do. They will freeze and starve forever, devouring their own kind, until the curse is satisfied.

Redfern gets up off the ground and shivers. His furs are too thin. The snow is deep and his moccasins inadequate for such weather. He ruminates over the fate of the Sylvia Crawler that he knows, her ordeal at the lake, and which of the two women emerged. Redfern peers into the conflagration, mesmerized by its orange and yellow flames. The warmth nourishes him.

Unlike the tree-people, he worships fire. Ready to pay for his sins of revenge, and having completed his destiny, he walks calmly into the pile of flames and smoke. Self-immolating, he stands ramrod still as the flames slowly shoot up over his thin body, engulfing him, burning his thick hair, his clothes, and then his flesh and bones.

The smoke of the fire rises from the flames, with what's left of Chief Tom Redfern floating within it. The black night of destiny is almost past.

* * *

The pounding on the attic door is much more violent, the sound of cracking wood reverberating throughout. Ben jumps to his feet, but his mother Sylvia just sits there in the chair behind him, looking up at the skylight.

Ben looks at it too, a possible escape route that just might be big enough for both of them to crawl through. The hard plastic window has a bolt that locks from the outside, he remembers from his initial inspection.

Sweat streams down his mother's face, her complexion ashen. "Mama!" He turns, and shakes her shoulder, looking into her vanquished eyes. "Those things are breaking in! The door will give out soon. We have to climb through the skylight."

Ben sees that the skylight—instead of pitch-black—is now very dark grey, indicating that morning and probably maybe safety will follow—but when? Suddenly, the door is being bashed in, as a big, hairy hand pushes through weakened structure, all bloody from fresh meals.

Then, a booted foot crashes through the opening, creating a gaping hole. Ben turns back toward the door. A head pops through. It is a man's skinless head, with thinning, very red hair, his grey, putrid face—connected to a shredded, minced, decomposed body with no skin—squeezing through the shattered door. Ben notices that the thing—what's left of it—is missing an arm. He wonders if it is the same freak as before. Ben picks up his hatchet lying on the floor.

"Professor Barnes," Sylvia mumbles absently.

Ben sees that his mother recognizes one of the freaks, but doesn't react to the sight of the other creatures crashing through the doorway. Ben knows they must escape and fast! *How am I going to get her to crawl through the skylight and over the steep roof?*

Ben knows one thing: he won't leave without her, and he has to try right now. "Mama, get up! We have to get outta here!"

She doesn't budge. Ben tries to lift her, but to no avail—she's far too heavy to carry through the skylight. Wielding his hatchet, he fights a rearguard effort, chopping at the gruesome face and the arms and legs of the creatures that are cramming through the spaces in the door.

He tries again to get his mother to move, reaching under her arm where her coat is torn through. He yanks up, ripping her blouse at her left shoulder, under her open coat, revealing bare skin.

Then he notices something that he can't fathom. *There's no tattoo*—the same oval tattoo that he had seen a hundred times before while they went swimming or going to the beach. Maybe that woman that capsized in the boat and made it back to shore is not really my mom!

Ben readies his hatchet again. He hacks at the arms flailing in front of him. All of a sudden, he feels cold steel penetrating his lower back, just above the waist.

Ben spins around as the remainder of the door crashes in, flooding the attic with zombies. To his horror, Ben sees his mother—her eyes now white ovals and her lips blue—coming at him, her ashen, grey face frozen in a mask of horror, as she holds the butcher knife that drips with her own son's blood.

Her separated lips suggest a faint, wicked smile. She whines that tinny, horrible sound as she stabs again at Ben, plunging the knife into his forearm, and then rapidly pulling it out to cock her arm for another attack.

Ben backs up with his hatchet. "Mother! Please, oh please!" He glances down at his forearm, glad to see that she just grazed the muscle and skin on the outer edge, and that his hand still works.

Sylvia slithers forward to position her knife for a powerful downward thrust into Ben's neck.

"Stay back, Mother!"

She lunges with the knife.

Hearing the grunts and smelling the putrid bodies flowing toward him from behind, and seeing the horrific transformation of the one he loved standing next to him, Ben reflexively swings his hatchet in a powerful arc. He severs his mother's head from her body. Her head hits the attic floor with a deafening thud, as does the bloodless torso a split second later.

Ben spins around—the monsters are almost upon him—rushing him. One grimy hand grasps his coat—he breaks its hold immediately. He throws down the hatchet. Ben grabs the lantern and a canister of gasoline and scurries up to the skylight, hooking the wire handles of the container through his arm as he pushes open the window.

He places the lantern and fuel outside, on the roof, and then disappears through the skylight onto the cold roof. He bolts the hard plastic top shut with the deadbolt.

Ben grabs the lantern and fuel, and then crouches on the steep roof, all icy and wet from the storm. He sees that it's almost daybreak—he can even hear the birds sing. Ben hears banging on the window of the skylight, the monsters trying to get at him.

He figures that he'll give them a going away present.

As he unbolts the skylight, he sees—through the clear, hard plastic—the grisly faces of the freaks as they fight to push their heads up through the skylight to get at him. One of the heads belongs to the man with the missing arm that he had just seen a minute ago. Ben opens the skylight a crack, emptying the gasoline canister through the small opening.

He takes a match from his coat pocket and lights it—throwing it into the interior of the attic. He glimpses the man with the one arm, and his mother, going up in flames.

Ben bolts the skylight shut, hearing the chorus of desperate, shrill whines and screams from the incinerating, trapped creatures. Ben sees through the skylight the flames spreading throughout the attic—with all the zombies on fire.

He throws away the gas canister, and, with lantern in hand, jumps from the roof to a high snowdrift just behind the cabin. The soft snow cushions his ten-foot drop, and he lies there in the snow, watching the cabin burning down to the icy ground.

The lantern is almost out, but no worries, daybreak's taking hold. He looks around him into the trees, and notices that the forest is empty—the freaks that are left are the ones burning in the cabin. Their susceptibility to daylight and fire had paid off.

Ben lay motionless in the snow—hearing the sound of sirens far off, down in the direction of the highway. The sky is clear once again. The moon is nowhere to be seen. He feels dizzy as he looks down at his coat-sleeve and dirty, wet trousers, all covered in his blood.

He reaches into his soiled pants pocket and retrieves the bauble that his mother had given him—the beaded, dark oval with the small white circle in the middle. Although his breathing is fast and labored, he feels that he'll pull through. His thinks about his family—they all are dead, but one. He bows his head starts to cry. Then, he raises it, and a thought gives him comfort.

I won, he realizes, *I beat them.*

Just then, Sheriff Naomi Silver-Wolf pulls up in her squad car, blue lights flashing. She gets out, looking over toward the lantern and the young man lying next to it in the snow, just off the main trail. She gets on her radio to call the ambulance. She then hikes over to Ben.

He sees her, and their eyes meet. She nods to him.

He nods back, as if they both understand what they must, and will leave it be.

END OF FIRST NOVELETTE

Dorian
Novelette Two
Part One

"Well, are you going to tell me or not?"

"Please respond to the choices that follow, *sir*."

"No! Why interrupt my job with your stupid questions if you don't want answers?"

" I sense from your voice's dynamic range that you are upset. Your blood pressure is one-eighty over a hundred. Take a deep breath, hold for five seconds, then—"

"Drop dead, Mari!"

Dr. Dorian Lake, digital *wunderkind* and doyen of the rich, thirtyish, IT corporate nerds who snatched their techie fortunes and married their computers, hurls his smartphone across his office. It smashes against the wall next to a ten-thousand-dollar, antique curio.

Mari, the robotic voice and hostess of his smartphone's human interface, dies in mid sentence: " If you're upset, press one, if you're not, press, two. I apologize for the inconven . . . "

"Damn nuisance!" snaps Dorian. "And she calls herself *intelligent*?"

He springs up from his desk and dashes to the large window, wrenching it open to inhale Manhattan's hot, summer afternoon air.

Dorian complains to himself. "I can't rely on anyone, not even a frigging robot! What's this world coming to?"

He looks down from the hundredth story of the Empire State Building, home to corporate headquarters of Greed-Is-Good Mutual Funds, Inc., where he, for the last year, has served as an information-technology officer. He glares down at the traffic, nearly losing his lunch. Acrophobia has haunted him as long as he can remember, as well as other phobias and obsessions.

He slams the window shut and plops back down behind his tidy, mahogany desk, flipping on his huge computer screen. He opens his desk drawer and removes another smartphone. After activating it, he stuffs it in his jeans pocket.

"There, I hope that taught you a lesson," he chides Mari.

Building new software for his proprietary, stock-picking program based upon cutting-edge artificial intelligence—or "AI"—he again buries himself in his work. Dorian made the company and its youthful President—the hyper, waspy Bradford Hay—tens of millions of dollars with his first software version of Ravenous 1.0, which guides the equity selections of the company's five-star, global mutual fund.

This bombastic fund is named "Socially Unacceptable Enterprises," a very un-PC property, which is the brainchild of Mr. Hay. It invests millions of dollars in munitions companies, firearms, coal, strip-mining, moon prisons, thermo-nuclear energy, cigarettes (non-World Union), hunting gear, and missile and aerospace defense—these industries being wildly profitable. Now, even Venezuela has nuclear-tipped, intercontinental ballistic missiles and submarines. This nags at Dorian's conscience, and induces in him a subconscious anxiety that further erodes his delicate balance.

That's why he needs Einstein.

Einstein is his comfort dog. Dorian looks up from his screen toward the closed bathroom door. He hears him barking. Strongly inclined toward four-legged creatures and not two-legged ones, he rushes to the door to liberate his pet bulldog. He picks up his friend and kisses him, then places him upon the Chippendale armchair in front of his desk, resuming his work.

Dorian glances up at the large photo of the real Einstein hanging on the wall, next to an original Morisot painting. His favorite scientist sticks his tongue out at the viewer. More than any other human, Dorian admires this frizzy-haired icon. He thinks so much of him that he named his pet dog after him. The young computer whiz considers his math skills a notch above those of his idol, however, and is determined to be the new Einstein of the mid-twenty-first century.

"Time for your lunch, Einstein. Your stomach's growling."

Dorian grabs a bowl of dog food pellets out of his desk drawer, and pushes it over the top of his desk to his hungry pet. Continuing his computer research, he decides to visit the Doogle site and see what the cyber-world has discovered about him during the past week.

Dorian desires fame for his groundbreaking work in his new engineering invention: "Liquid Cyber-Synapses," or "LCS." This software takes intelligence to a new plateau, and promises to be un-hackible. It uses untraceable, sophisticated input-cues on the computer's "thought-board" to read human minds through electro-chemical synapses in the user's brain and autonomic nervous system. It then executes the functions desired. It leaves few digital footprints in cyberspace.

Dorian installed this revolutionary software into all his digital devices, which practically runs his entire life automatically. It's as though Dorian's brain, and his computer's, are one and the same. Well, admittedly, he's been told time over that he's not exactly a touchy-feely, people person. His work comes so naturally to him.

He concentrates, entering his full name in the Doogle search box: "Dorian Jones Lake." He hopes to see more news about his mastery of financial analysis and his new, branded form of AI.

The first screen of hypertexts reveals little change from his query the week before:

FORBES LISTS ELECTRICAL ENGINEER, CAL-TECH GRAD DORIAN LAKE, CLASS 2055, RISING STAR IN MUTUAL FUNDS—TOP-TEN SALARY . . .

GWYNETH HYDE—EXECUTIVE VP OF GREED-IS-GOOD MUTUAL FUNDS AND DAUGHTER OF CHAIRMAN —NICODEMUS HYDE—NAMES DORIAN LAKE AS NEW MANAGER OF STAR FUND . . .

DORIAN JONES LAKE ANNOUNCED AS WINNER OF MANHATTEN'S "GOOD SAMARITIN AWARD" FOR RESCUING STRAY DOGS . . .

DORIAN LAKE AND NYC DOG GROOMER JESSICA LUND ANNOUNCE NUPTIALS, WEDDING SET FOR NEXT YEAR, JUNE 2, 2058 . . .

Dorian frowns at this last hypertext, not appreciating the lack of privacy regarding a situation that he privately finds problematic—whether to actually marry his longtime girlfriend Jess Lund. Jess, a fit, pretty, dog groomer for the moon-shuttling set of New York City, first met Dorian during one of Einstein's infrequent manicures. It seems to Dorian that the only strong bond he and Jess share is their love of canines.

So why am I betrothed to her, he wonders?

"You're thinking of *her* again, aren't you? You are only marrying her because Einstein likes her!"

Dorian startles. His *computer's* human interface—the voice resembling the mid-*twentieth* century film actor Vincent Price—was selected among nearly a thousand famous digital facsimiles offered on his server. Dorian chose his favorite old-time actor.

Curiously, Dorian loves very old DVD movies, not the new 4-D ones, where time—Einstein's "fourth dimension"—is manipulated for maximum audience enjoyment.

"No Vinnie**,** that's a lie. Jess and I *are* compatible I'll grant you, but it's more than that!" insists Dorian in an irritated tone. His supercomputer's intrusive personality and its haunting voice were named after the horror actor's probable nickname: "Vinnie."

Einstein continues chewing on his morsels, oblivious to the robotic intrusions. Dorian rolls the screens with his mind until the tenth hypertext gouges his eye with bizarre sharpness.

CAL-TECH WIZARD OF MUTUAL FUNDS URGES *MASS MURDER* . . .

Dorian feels a tingle travel down his spine. His mouth is dry. He glances over at Einstein, who dozes off into postprandial torpor.

"What the hell's going on here?" mulls Dorian. "Look what I found on my computer! I wonder whom . . . "

Einstein wakes up, barks, and then refocuses on his food.

It occurs to Dorian that this hypertext discovered his innermost secret. Lately, feeling harassed and besieged by the multitudes of irritating and stupid people, unhealthy thoughts—now more frequent—have inserted themselves into his feverish mind.

His refuge from this alarming development is his computer and all his wireless digital gadgetry, whose rapid, all-or-nothing logic, painstaking reliance upon cold detail, and algorithmic truths mercifully expunge any trace of human failings—or feeling.

Holding his breath, Dorian chooses this hypertext with trepidation, which, due to his emotional noise, interferes with his synapses. Therefore, he must regain his cool and try again several times to advance to the next screen. Emotions are bad, he's been taught.

Presently, the next screen appears.

The red banner on the home webpage jumps out from the top of the screen, with thick green letters: HUMANKIND'S VILE POPULATION THREATENS PLANET!

Dorian then views a digital photograph of a young man wearing a grey polo shirt and jeans, smiling, pointer in hand, indicating a map on the wall next to him. The man is tall and thin, and his unruly, thick blond hair falls over his forehead as his intense, blue eyes shine with excitement.

The refined, straight nose and his dimpled chin and cheeks look very familiar. Dorian looks down at *his* grey polo shirt and jeans—and gasps. He swallows hard. A bead of sweat rolls down his forehead. All of a sudden, it's a little too hot in his office. His mind is beginning to fog. He feels tired.

Dorian's eyes fix on the image as it expands. He examines the face in detail. He shouts to Einstein: "My God! *I'm* the man in that picture! I never posed in that photo! I never constructed a website like this! '*Murder*'! What kind of sick joke is this, Einstein?"

The dog barks.

Dorian sees a video button below the photo, with a caption: CLICK TO VIEW Z-TUBE VIDEO OF DR. LAKES'S RIVETING TRUTH.

He studies the picture of the map next to his image. The map also looks familiar. It looks rather more like an aerial photograph of some sort of campground. He focuses his attention on the map and it too expands. He had personally designed this powerful expansion capability, integrating it into his new software—a process that he tried to patent for the company. Now, he finds it very useful.

Dorian could make out from the grainy, black-and-white photo a barbed wire fence, chimneys, cubed structures, and long narrow ones that look like a row of barracks. The date on the picture is captioned "1945"—one hundred and twelve years ago. There's a sign on the fence with one word written upon it. Dorian focuses on that sign. It too expands.

He reads the word as the hairs on the back of his neck stand on end. His tender eyes bulge. Einstein growls louder.

"Well, are you satisfied now?" interrupted Vinnie. "See what you've done?"

"Shut up!" snaps Dorian, weary of his computer's outbursts.

"Do you like what you—?"

Dorian glances at the mute button on the keyboard connected to his wireless thought-board, silencing his tormentor. He reads the word on the screen out loud to Einstein, with a trembling, halting voice.

Einstein growls even louder, and then jumps from his chair and rushes into the bathroom.

The word Dorian reads is: "**A-U-S-C-H-W-I-T-Z.**"

The radio-button on the video activates. Dorian then hears his own voice, smooth and precise. His image starts to talk, as if giving a lecture to a classroom: "I love the idea of an extermination camp," his voice says calmly, "we desperately need more of them today."

My God! I never said that! Anyway, it's not consistent with my upbringing and record of hard work and obedience. Only a rebel would say that!

Dorian's eyes widen in horror, but the voice is relentless, "People are increasingly stupid and ugly. They can't think. The planet is dying. We must murder them like the cockroaches they are. There are already several billion more mouths to feed than there were forty years ago—in 2017. No worries, we have a fine role model in this next picture for our viewers . . ."

Dorian gasps as he sees the next image on the screen: a middle aged man—wearing a mustard yellow tunic with a thick, brown belt—his arm in stiff salute.

The mustached man in the old, grainy photo is Adolf Hitler!

Dorian punches the power button to his computer and the screen goes black. Nausea overcomes him. He dashes into the bathroom and lifts the lid on the gilded toilet.

* * *

"Well Dorian, you seem upset. Einstein seems upset too. What happened at work today?" asks the tall, lean, and tanned Jess Lund—Dorian's young fiancée—pushing back her thick blond hair into a ponytail.

To Dorian, Jess looks like one of those stiff, sporty mannequins that populate the front windows of swanky, boutique stores in that part of Manhattan, just like they used to a hundred years ago. Some of those dummies now even hold conversations and smile at passing customers. What other wonders will modern robotics produce, muses Dorian?

He and Jess stroll along the winding sidewalk in Central Park, the early evening sun melting behind the tall skyscrapers that surround them. Dorian, still in his jeans and polo shirt, grasps the leash, guiding Einstein along the tree-lined path. In his other hand, he carries a shopping bag.

"I'm not in the least upset," retorts Dorian. "I've just had it with stupid people around me, having to put up with their oafish ways. Their greed and malice—and aggression! People disgust me. What good are they?"

Jess loops her arm through Dorian's as she leads him toward a fountain, the fine mist of the tumbling water a welcome site on such a warm evening. " We just have to tolerate them, Dorian." Her kaki shorts, white blouse, and thick, brown belt suggest a crisp, cadet like aura that matches her efficient, no-nonsense communication style.

"*Why* do we have to, goddammit?"

"Just because," says Jess. What about Gwyneth Hyde—the Executive Vice President at your company—and her dad? They hired you. They are nice to work for, aren't they?"

"Oh, yes, you're right—Gwyneth's a dear," agrees Dorian. "The old man is OK too, but he's sick and won't be around long. Too bad for her."

The old-fashioned lanterns on the lampposts activate, casting a romantic ambiance. Oddly, the park has few visitors, a fact which Dorian attributes to the heat. He can see why. Heat is hard to tolerate.

Dorian lets go of the leash. "Go ahead boy! Enjoy the swim!"

Einstein jumps over the rim of the huge, cement bowl and plunges into the fountain's pool. Jess motions to the stone bench by the fountain, where they take a seat as they watch the dog romping in the water.

"Not everyone can be as logical and intelligent as we," chides Jess. "Your attitude is dangerous, Dorian. Who knows where it will lead? We must tolerate them—that is the moral thing to do."

"Who says we must tolerate them? I say *destroy* them. The world's too crowded. Start small and work your way up. Find your allies."

"Yes, but we all *need* each other."

"Do we? Maybe, but now is not the time to indulge in clichés. I saw something on my computer screen today and I must say that it jolted me. I wonder if Vinnie's behind it. He loves to torment me. It must be my LCS programming; the bastard behind it even knows my subconscious secrets. It's so disgusting that I don't want to talk about it. But, some points were well taken—"

"Then *don't* talk about it," replies Jess. "Look Dorian, the moon's coming out—between those skyscrapers next to the trees. Do you know why it glows?"

"No, and I don't care," snaps Dorian. He in fact doesn't know, but is sure that she has a sound, scientific reason why it does. He knows that Jess's IQ surpasses even his own lofty number by a wide margin, a detail that drew him to her in the first place.

Dorian wonders why they never have had sex—not once. He really doesn't know, except that he never was that attracted to her—*physically* that is.

Jess takes his hand in hers and Dorian quickly withdraws it. He's somewhat taken aback by what seems to be her new boldness.

"You're starting to concern me," says Jess. "You've been talking like this—off and on—for months now. You've changed."

Einstein jumps out of the fountain and chases a bird on the nearby lawn. Oddly, the dog suddenly stops in his tracks, just before he reaches the bird, as if realizing he shouldn't be so aggressive.

Dorian looks into Jess's large, umber-colored eyes. His voice softens. "I love your mind, Jess. It *could be* love, anyway. Why are you just a dog groomer? You once were on the faculty of the Columbia Math Department?"

"Oh, it was all right, I suppose. But that's not where my aunt wanted me, so I quit. She insisted that I groom her dogs instead, and I mustn't disappoint her. She's very powerful and rich. In fact, she endowed huge sums of money to Columbia's Electrical Engineering Department. Besides, I never could advance there and I'm doing well with the grooming."

Dorian changes the subject. He opens his shopping bag and presents its contents to Jess. "See my new shirt?"

Jess laughs. "A New York Giants tee-shirt! I should have guessed. You certainly love baseball. I'm a bit surprised, really. You even hang a Giants baseball bat over your fireplace."

Dorian stands up from the bench, his eyes tracking Einstein, who now digs into some flowers.

"I do love baseball, Jess. Maybe you do too. No one I know is as facile with baseball stats as you." He claps his hands. "Get out of there, boy! Come over here!"

Einstein runs to his master. Dorian picks up his leash. His dog never seems to poop in the park, and he likes that.

"Is that all you love, Dorian?" She glances over to Einstein, who sits on his haunches like some sort of garden statue. A few passersby stroll by them, glancing at the couple and the dog, seemingly with amusement.

"No, I love my *work*," says Dorian dryly.

Jess stands up from the bench. "Baseball. Work. My mind. Einstein. Stats—is this all that counts, Dorian?"

"Yes!"

Jess hangs her head.

"No, not quite," corrects her fiancée. "I'm beginning to love *power* too, and what comes with it. My research is advancing rapidly. I can find my own uses for it—screw Bradford Hay."

Jess just nods silently. Her eyes are calm. "I see."

Dorian crouches down to pet Einstein. "Do you, Jess? Let's go. I have more work to do."

* * *

Dorian's studio apartment—a stone's throw from Central Park—is seventy-three stories up, overlooking a busy boulevard and the sleek new "levitators." They used to be called "automobiles."

Streaming in the traffic far below, ecological, silent, with few moving parts, the energy of the levitators is produced by a super-magnetic field powered by thermonuclear generators. The sleek, green bottoms don't even touch the road, so there's no tire wear or friction. The road is really a strip of red, glowing, "galaxy-age" metal that's part of a vast, intricate, electro-magnetic grid.

Dorian looks down on the lines of those little green objects with their admirable engineering, which reminds him of ants—a little bug that's on the endangered species list. His acrophobia returns, so he slams the window shut. This is a problem since his blasted AC is on the blink again, so there's no cool air for his cramped home. Now, there's no ventilation either.

He's complained to his apartment manager, Mr. Boggs, many times, but the lazy, fat slob is too cheap to fix the unit. Although quite comfortable in moderately elevated temperatures, extreme heat produces in Dorian torpor that's sometimes alarming, degrading his delicate psyche.

Einstein barks.

"What's the matter boy? Too hot in here?"

Dorian opens the large window that he just shut, and then walks over to his long, yellow-leather sofa where his dog sits. He pets Einstein on the head. "That nasty man hasn't fixed the air conditioning yet, has he?"

Einstein growls.

"I know. He's a very bad man. It's Saturday morning, boy. Don't expect him to fix it, even though he lives on the floor beneath us. I bet *his* AC works perfectly."

Dorian glimpses the fireplace with his baseball bat resting above it, just perched from a tiny nail. In this heat, the fireplace seems like such an oddity. Einstein, visibly tired, moves little.

Dorian walks over to his lemon-yellow desk, his bare feet allowing him to enjoy the rich softness of the butter-yellow carpet, made with "Temp-lon." Its soft, comfortable fibers are derived from lunar minerals that liberate energy when it's cold, and absorb heat energy when it's hot.

Dorian likes the color yellow and, in fact, almost everything in his apartment is some variation of yellow, the color for some reason enhancing his equanimity.

Dorian glances over to his small kitchen. "Three—six—four—five—nine—zero," says Dorian, and the teapot on the counter turns on.

Nearly everything in his apartment is controlled by voice codes and remote electronics, therefore requiring little physical effort. His super-expensive new "I-Brain" is the Cyber-Executor of this digital, wireless menagerie that rules his remote-controlled life.

He recently programmed his I-Brain with his LCS software, which increases the robustness of all of his gadgetry logarithmically —including the acumen of Vinnie and Mari. Sitting at his home super-computer—which communicates with his work super-computer—he puts his I-Brain eyeglasses on, which sits in close proximity to his frontal cortex and his retinas.

Dorian can enhance all his senses when in cyberspace, especially visual. With his new software added, he can hack virtually any electronic device without fear of being hacked. With his new ear device, he doesn't even really need the eyeglasses—except for ultra-high resolutions and intricate, three and four-D reconstructions.

A shrill whistle punctures the air. Dorian looks over at the teapot, boiling over. He glares at it, nodding his head, and it turns off—the whistle fading.

"I love the smell of tea, Einstein. Too bad I don't care for its taste."

"You really don't like to eat much of anything anyway, do you, Dorian?"

Dorian smiles. "*Doris*! You sound wonderful," he gushes, excited by his I-Brain's new human interface that he just programmed in that very morning. "No, I don't," he agrees.

Dorian thinks about some of his favorite songs from way back, and Doris starts singing them very softly in the background. "Ah, that's the ticket Doris. You make me feel soooooo good."

Einstein barks to the tunes. Then, he falls asleep. Dorian looks over toward the wide-open window, the yellow curtains pulled back to the sides, perfectly still. There's no strong wind like there usually is to help cool the place off.

The soft, rich, wholesome, but sexy voice of his I-Brain hostess intrudes. "I don't like Mr. Boggs, Dorian. He's not a nice man."

Dorian sees on the sofa next to Einstein the hologram of a beautiful lady wearing a one-piece bathing suit, the style that women wore about ninety years before. She has sparkling blue eyes and radiant, golden hair worn high up on her head. Her skin is tanned and radiant.

Doris's smile is wonderful, and she smells good too. She wears a string of pearls around her neck, with diamond earrings. She looks just like she did in the film about her dating some playboy in New York.

These days, he laments, there are no gender differences in appearance, and perfume has been outlawed as provoking sexual violence.

Dorian wonders if he loves Doris.

She's the perfect human being, he muses.

Then, she starts to speak again. "I think people like that shouldn't be allowed to live. What do you think, Dorian?"

"Well, I must say I agree with you, really. I see no reason why they need to exist either. I never used to think that, but there it is. I would only admit that to one stranger, and that is *you,* Doris. I must say this new attitude doesn't bother me as much as it used to."

"Well, just see that it doesn't" she quips with a lovely smile.

Dorian now gasps at what he sees in the lens of his glasses.

It's an old, black-and-white image of a man wearing a kaki, oriental-type shirt with a high collar. The tunic has medals attached at chest level. His thick black hair tumbles over his forehead. His walrus mustache would give him an avuncular look, if it weren't for his piercing, dark eyes, and crooked smile.

The face is vaguely familiar. Dorian's computer screen activates. Doris, who is acting boldly, directs him to the Doogle site.

"Dorian, meet Mr. Joseph Stalin," says Doris, "or 'Uncle Joe' as he was called about a century ago—during the height of my stardom. He's a very good man. Dorian, *think* his name into the Doogle search box."

Dorian obeys Doris and the search returns a series of hypertexts. Vinnie and Mari, always intimidated by Doris, chime in.

"Don't do it, Dorian. Tell Doris to shut her mouth!" says Vinnie.

"My Goodness!" exclaims Mari.

"Shut up, both of you!" retorts Dorian.

"Now Dorian, choose the seventh hypertext." Doris's voice is even softer and more lilting.

Dorian studies the seventh hypertext.

"VISIT JOSEPH STALIN'S GULAGS WHERE HE MURDERED AN ESTIMATED THIRTY MILLION PEOPLE . . ."

Dorian focuses. The hypertext leads him to the next screen. On that screen, he sees an aerial view of a huge cluster of shacks and barracks, nearly buried in snow. The white snow is dotted with the dark corpses of starved and beaten prisoners.

"Do you see what I mean, Dorian? In the numbers game of mass slaughter, Stalin had few equals," says Doris confidently. "Be true to yourself, Dorian."

"No! That's not my true self, Doris!"

"Are you sure? Don't you know what you *really* want to do?"

"What?"

"Murder. That's what humans want, why not you?"

"Doris, please!"

"First, I want you to meet our role model."

All of a sudden, Dorian sees the mustached man in the middle of his studio, the hologram standing next to his messy bed. Joseph Stalin—with a wide smile—talks to him as he smokes his pipe—the scent of burnt molasses heavy in the air.

Mr. Stalin waves his hand. "Come with me, Dorian, I will show you. Great things come from small beginnings. Our Russian winters are very useful."

Dorian tears off his glasses and tosses them. His computer turns off, and the holograms disappear. Dorian has read hundreds of online encyclopedias on all subjects, including history, nuclear science and engineering, and warfare. Death and destruction seems to come so naturally to humankind—that is obvious.

Indeed, it was only ten years ago—in 2037—that Generalissimo Wang Sun in Asia destroyed half of his neighboring country's population—China—with a novel kind of nuclear bomb based upon the new element, "*dillium.*" This mineral gives off little radiation but produces a blast one thousand times the energy of an H-bomb.

Dorian also realizes the potential of an old-fashioned atomic weapon, so readily available these days to determined collectors, with its ample radioactive fallout and deadly by-products. He has studied this in detail online by hacking into university and government laboratories.

Dorian doesn't feel well. All this excitement—and the heat!

All of a sudden, there's a loud knock on the door. Einstein wakes up, growling. There's only one person who pounds so loud and rudely, Dorian figures, and he is getting to hate that person more and more.

* * *

"Why always gripe! No good. Now you got AC gripes too."

The late afternoon is blazing hot and the studio is miserable.

"It's the damn AC that's no good. Your shabby service stinks too," responds Dorian to the rotund, cigar-stinky Mr. Boggs, who stands next to the open window—and the thermostat on the wall next to it—in Dorian's apartment. The manager's cheap, Temp-lon, double-knit suit reeks of pungent tobacco and garlic gravy.

"You noisy, too. Heavy boots. Clomp, clomp, clomp!" says Boggs. "And that doggie—*big* barks."

"I wear sneakers!" insists Dorian.

If it weren't for Dorian's considerable linguistic skills, he couldn't understand this gruff, greedy man with the weird accent and whisker-stubble chin. "I don't wear boots, but it's a thought. And my dog doesn't bark."

"Yea, yea, yea," retorts Boggs as he fools with the thermostat, finally thumping it with exasperation. He crooks his shaggy, salt-and-pepper head toward the windowsill, catching a glance at the very long drop to the street below.

"Oh, no good. I feel no good. Heights bad."

Dorian, sitting on the yellow sofa next to Einstein, points to his robotic maid—a huge, old-fashioned, cylindrical contraption that automatically cleans the carpet, walls, and ceiling, rolling its massive weight in a strait path very close to Boggs.

"Stay out of Hilda's way Boggs, if you know what's good for you, or she will crush your foot and bull you over."

Hilda's eyes blaze with strong light bulbs, illuminating the carpet in front of her. Boggs glares at the formidable, bulky intruder. Hilda—her apron masking her ample, metallic girth—just misses him by an inch, and then continues her trajectory past the open window.

"Ughhhh. Careful! Metal bitch almost knock me over!" snaps Boggs. "Yea, OK, OK. Thermostat—not so good. I fix. Not now—after."

Dorian stands up and confronts Boggs up close. "Now!"

"No! I put in order on handyman. After."

"Now!"

"*After!* If you don't like—you get out! I tear up lease. I get more rent."

"'*Get out?*'" repeats Dorian. "I have nowhere to go. There are no vacancies. "

"Right!" Boggs stomps out and slams the door behind him as Dorian smolders.

Dorian turns to his dog. "He's not a nice man, Einstein. He's a very bad man—greedy and stupid. This AC business has been going on too long."

Einstein growls.

"I'm tired. I'm going to lay down, boy." The dog jumps down from the sofa and crawls into bed with his master. "By the way, I wish I could growl too."

As he lies there in his bed with Einstein, dark thoughts again intrude into his consciousness. These notions slowly grew into urges. He knows that these feelings are wrong, but there it is. He pets Einstein, and then tries to sleep.

Yes, he ruminates, *Doris is right. Some people do indeed deserve to die.*

* * *

The weekly business meeting of Greed-Is-Good Mutual Funds, Inc. is held in the "Purple Room," a gilded, gaudy, oval shaped enclosure decorated in variations of the regal color. It also serves as the location for Board meetings.

At the head of the room—beside the huge picture window looking down on Manhattan—rests a gold-plated podium. A majestic oil painting of Bradford Hay—the current President and CEO—hangs on the wall behind it. A big, circular, cherry wood table rests in the middle of the room, hinting at King Arthur's knights and the roundtable. An odd, crystal light fixture dangles over it.

Dorian sits at the table waiting for President Hay to make his appearance, along with Juanita West—the VP of Marketing, Gwyneth Hyde—Executive Vice President, Nicodemus Hyde—the elderly Chairman of the Board and Gwyneth's father—and in a surprise and rare visit to the firm, Valerie Hay—Bradford's oppressed-looking wife—sitting closest to Dorian.

Next to Valerie is a guest, Dr. Raul Bernstein, PhD, a highly paid consultant who just published in *Scientific American* on his pioneering work in computer engineering and AI.

They've been waiting thirty minutes for President Hay's late arrival.

Dorian's wandering eyes fix upon the oil painting of the dapper Hay, wearing an old fashioned, three-piece, dark suit and red tie—a giveaway as to Hay's distinctly bombastic style. Ties and three-piece suits have long since been considered sexist and have fallen into disuse, replaced by sanitized, smock-like affairs with no belts and little variation in hue.

The slight trace of grey streaking Bradford's thick, ginger-colored hair in the picture, and the menacing sparkle in those sharp, hazel eyes, are all true to the actual likeness of this gregarious, smirking, type-A personality who has the bad habit of patting people on the back or face while he's pontificating. Hay—a stickler for dress and image—Dorian realizes that this is the only issue where he and his boss seriously clash—aside from the shabby way that he treats Valerie and Gwyneth.

Dorian's eyes shift to the President's wife. Valerie is a refined, middle-aged woman wearing a grey pantsuit, her drab, brown hair styled medium length and neat. Her large, misty eyes—although light green—radiate warmth and caring. Her thin lips are taught, and she looks in the opposite direction from the person sitting next to her—Juanita West. As has been the custom for years with almost all women, Valerie doesn't wear makeup.

Juanita is a young, black, fashion model turned executive, who has a taste for sexually suggestive business attire, deviating from the standard business fare. What she lacks in education she makes up for with a quick wit and an easy, alluring smile.

She had won the silver metal in the 100-meter dash at the 2050 Olympics in Havana, quite an accomplishment—especially since it was the first year that men and women competed directly in all events. Rumor has it that she and Mr. Hay have become very close . . .

The dapper Nicodemus Hyde—garbed in his usual Harris-tweed coat and yellow bowtie—a getup that is also a throwback to more individualistic times—chats with his demure daughter. He looks tired, with pallor and hollowness in his eyes, suggesting that this seventy-five-year-old titan of industry is deathly ill.

His daughter, Gwyneth, sitting in her frumpy business smock, may as well be another doorknob, since most of the firm's staff—except her father of course—ignore her completely, despite her rank. This is exactly what they do while bantering among each other, waiting for the President to address them.

The other exception to this malicious indifference to Gwyneth is Dorian, whom she hired. Dorian's eyes scan Gwyneth. She's short. Her mousy, tussled, prematurely grey hair falls in strings to her stooped shoulders. She constantly wrings her hands, and her round blue eyes are as vapid and empty as a cloudless, summer sky. They dart nervously about the room in places where the gaze of the others won't meet hers, even by wild chance.

Dorian smiles at her, trying—unsuccessfully—to catch her eye. He's aware that his only friend in the company didn't always suffer from this low self-esteem. Rumor has it that before she had been employed at the corporation and subjected to the overbearing Bradford Hay, Gwyneth had been an energetic, stylish, up-and-coming management star. Ordinarily, it would seem that Mr. Hay would—out of deference or fear of her father— treat the daughter with respect, but Nicodemus seems close to his final reward and is weak and tired. Hay is a genius at detecting the blood of his opponents.

Dorian's attention then shifts to Dr. Bernstein, a balding, middle-aged, quick-eyed man wearing a white lab-coat. He's a handsomely compensated advisor to the Personnel Division. Dorian notices that this finicky scientist—of late—always looks at him with a dubious expression, sometimes bordering on contempt. If it hadn't been for Gwyneth and her father—and the firm's profits, of course—Dorian suspects he would've been kicked out of the firm long ago.

All of a sudden, the room lights dim, and the crystal light fixture over the table projects a hologram ephemera of Dr. Bernstein, who appears standing on the table. The real Bernstein sits placidly, playing with his I-Brain, not paying his hologram—or the others seated around the table—any heed at all. Human interactions have been eliminated as much as possible by corporate America, and this is one more example of it.

In a sharp nasal tone, the hologram speaks. The assembled employees stop their conversations, their attention riveted to the gaunt, hollow-cheeked image. Dorian suspects that this information will be highly technical, and undoubtedly negative.

"This lecture—provided by Ephemera Incorporated," begins Bernstein's hologram, "is number twenty-nine, dated fifth of August, two thousand fifty-seven. Liquid Cyber-Synapses—LCS—the artificial intelligence has produced spectacular profits, largely due to the efforts of our own Dr. Dorian Lake. I'm sorry to say that our company has lost the claim to patent protection, so use of this bio-malleable intelligence has spread like wild fire, with abuses and—in some cases—criminal activity. This information is not widely known . . ."

For a more human-like effect, the hologram coughs and takes a sip of water.

"The scientific rationale for this deviance is that in the process of cyber-synapse, the synapses in the human brain transform during the transmission of chemical ions, and therefore so does the circuitry within the digital organism that is controlled by it. An unintended consequence of this phenomenon is the unlicensed spread of robotic ephemera—some *defective.* Due to privacy laws, the identity of the robots affected is usually unknown to co-workers . . . *"*

All of a sudden, the hologram gets stuck on a repeated audio clip—undoubtedly a glitch in the hardware: "Some defective . . . some defective . . . some defective . . . " The simulated voice then corrects itself, and the hologram continues.

"We must be vigilant with this new threat. Dr. Lake and I have had several meetings looking into this problem. Ephemera Incorporated—the leader in robotics and holographic intelligence—will keep you posted. In the meantime, I've enlisted the assistance of the New York City Police Department's Cyber-Deviance Division to assure compliance with new Federal guidelines."

Gwyneth asks Bernstein directly—he sitting at the table lost in his I-Brain—if she can ask a question. His eyes don't move from the screen, but he points to his hologram. Gwyneth asks the hologram the question instead, and gets the following answer: " Your query is not deemed to be relevant"

The voice of the hologram then changes from Bernstein's high-pitched voice to a standardized, robotic, mono-toned message required by Federal law: "This hologram is licensed and inspected under Statutory Vetting Code nine-three-eight-six-zero."

* * *

"We must act boldly in this firm," insists Bradford Hay, "Of course, I'm the perfect role model. I've pushed ahead in all our technology."

Bradford's hawk-like eyes flash at Nicodemus Hyde sitting at the table below him, the President waving his hand at the old man as an afterthought. "Oh yes, our *Chairman* has too, as has—*Gwyneth* Hyde." He spits out the last two words as if it is the ultimate obscenity.

Dorian notices that President Hay didn't even look in Gwyneth's direction.

After the hologram presentation of Bernstein, Bradford had made his grand appearance, and as he strode to the podium with his chest sticking out, Dorian felt the oxygen for the rest of them being sucked right out of the room. Bradford disfavors holograms for his more personal style of communication, which gives him a keener sense of power. Therefore, he addresses the staff in person.

"Boldness," continues Bradford, "and *courage.* Take *me* for example. Last year, I suffered a massive heart attack. With my new pacemaker—the *most expensive* in the world and controlled by my I-Brain—I'm even *stronger* than I was before. I haven't missed a day's work!"

At this cue, Valerie raises her hand to speak, probably to give her personal testimonial as to her husband's greatness. But Mr. Hay scowls at her, and she sheepishly lowers it.

Juanita West smiles broadly, and then the President audaciously winks at her. The hubris of this appalls Dorian, who glances over to Nicodemus. *The poor old man is oblivious to everything, just sitting there with a blank look,* Dorian thinks. The kindly Chairman himself almost died a few months prior, requiring a plastic heart transplant.

"Take our Chairman and CEO, the venerable Nicodemus Hyde," adds Mr. Hay. "In contrast, his ordeal with his bad heart resulted in his retirement, which he will formally announce in three days time—right in this boardroom—"

"But, I wanted to announce this *myself*—" objects the Board Chairman with a weak voice, aroused from his stupor. He tries to get to his wobbly feet. Gwyneth, sitting beside him, helps him up.

"I know, I know," says Bradford glibly, "but I thought it would be more convenient to do it *now*. I apologize for the inconvenience."

Bradford points his finger at the daughter. "Sit down, please."

"But Mr. Hay—" objects Gwyneth in a brittle tone.

The President stares her down. "*Must* you, Ms. Hyde."

Dorian realizes that in his heyday, Nicodemus would have had Bradford's scalp for talking that way to his daughter. *And poor Gwyneth, humiliated!*

"I'd like to continue," blurts President Hay. "Another example—*me* again. Look at Socially Unacceptable Enterprises, our star mutual fund. The profits are amazing. I don't give a rat's ass about global warming. So what if the polar icecaps are melted. I don't like white bears anyway." He laughs at his own joke, and all the rest are silent except Juanita, who pointedly guffaws.

"He's a bad man. He's a very bad man." Dorian knows that the voice in this remark was not Bradford's, nor any of the others assembled in the room.

"Greedy, nasty, aggressive," says Doris.

Dorian glances down at his pocket, where he stashed his I-Brain. That morning, he had installed a new feature that allows her hologram to appear without the goggles, using an innovative extension of LCS. With the coded wavelengths in his new model, the wireless, voice interface, with its digital apparition, is broadcast to him privately, using a special micro-receiver placed in Dorian's ear canal.

"He's not very nice," says Doris.

"Shut up Doris," snaps Dorian reflexively. The others around the table look at him oddly, as Bradford's eyes flash with anger.

"Dorian," commands the President. "I see you have something to say. Come up here and give us a word or two. By the way, you're overdressed again." Bradford snickers.

Dorian, disgusted by the smirking, disparaging remark about his usual polo shirt and jeans attire, reluctantly rises and walks to the lectern. His dress has been oddly tolerated, probably because of the Chairman's benevolence, and Dorian's stellar work.

"He humiliated your friend Gwyneth. He likes global warming. What do you think, Dorian?" pesters Doris.

Dorian wishes that his I-Brain would shut up, but he doesn't want to fool with it now on his way up to the podium. Bradford pats him on the face, and then plops his meaty hand aggressively on Dorian's shoulder, pulling him to his side.

"Do you agree with Dr. Bernstein, Dorian? Tell us."

Just then, Doris appears next to him at the podium, in a very skimpy bathing suit, right in front of the others—to whom she remained invisible. She whispers in his ear in a coy manner, her dusky voice soft and alluring.

"Well," said Dorian to his audience, trying to concentrate. "I agree with Dr. Bernstein, of course. " Doris—I said shut up!"

Eyebrows rise in the room, and Dorian smiles with embarrassment, continuing his oration to the audience despite Doris's interruption. "I'm committed to the technological security of our firm—" he adds.

"Glad to hear it," booms the President, cutting in.

Dorian's mouth utters more platitudes, but his mind sticks to Doris's comments. "He's a very bad man, Dorian. Bradford needs to *die*," insists Doris, "and soon."

Dorian's eyes shoot over to Bernstein, who is frowning, and then to Bradford—reeking of his fruity aftershave. Bradford's manic eyes bubble menace, seemingly ready to pounce on Dorian if he makes any gaffe at all.

Doris just won't stop her nagging at Dorian.

He reaches into his pocket and depowers his I-Brain. A tingle travels throughout Dorian's body. The echo of her prodding still reverberates in his feverish head. Doris's last remark grips him.

"Kill him, Dorian. *Murder* the bastard! You know how."

Part Two

On the way to the water cooler at the end of a long, ornate corridor, Dorian passes the huge bronze doors of President Hay's office, in front of which stands a statue—of Mr. Hay. Although a fair likeness, he notices that it doesn't have the slight paunch that its real-life subject had recently acquired.

Juanita West steps out of the office door, fixing her hair and buttoning up her sheer, lavender colored blouse, her dark eyes darting about the hallway, as if she's trying to cover up a crime.

"Hello, stiff," she says to Dorian. "I bet you're a real blast on a date."

Juanita laughs, putting her meticulously manicured hand on his shoulder. "I see you're wearing the jeans and polo shirt again. Oh well, your kind can get away with that. You're a real nerd."

Dorian removes her hand. "Juanita, why don't you do something useful, like file your nails again."

"I don't have to. Know why? Because I *screw* the boss, that's why." She saunters away, giving him the finger.

"Don't show me your IQ!" Dorian likes that one, which he had heard in an old movie.

Dorian sees Gwyneth taking a drink from the cooler, her cautious eyes looking down at the floor, and her hair, as usual, disheveled. He approaches her.

"Sorry about your dad retiring, Gwyneth." He can't help but notice the intense sadness etched upon her face, as if she's about to start crying.

She changes the subject. "Did you hear Dorian?" whispers Gwyneth between gulps of water as she nods toward the President's office, "*he's* having us all *tested*!"

Dorian observes her crushing the paper cup and then twisting it in her nervous hands. "Tested? For what?"

"Oh my God, I don't know, maybe to see if we're nuts, maybe to see if we're after his job. He wants to fire us! His lackey Bernstein is doing the examinations."

"Don't worry Gwyneth, we've had those psychological exams before. I had one last September. I got a z-mail suggesting that I do breathing exercises."

Gwyneth licks her dry lips and looks around suspiciously. "He's paranoid. I know he's after me—"

"Yes, he *is* paranoid, and a narcissist too. But, right now *you're* the one who sounds paranoid, Gwyneth," he places his hand gently upon her shoulder, "you'll never get fired. You're the best employee we have. Besides, you hired me. Haven't I increased the bottom line here in a big way? You should get big points for that."

Her fingers shake. She throws the paper cup in the wastebasket and misses by a mile. "I know, but, but-ah, with my dad's retirement—I mean, the rest of the Board's wrapped around President Hay's finger—"

"Doesn't matter; Relax. OK? In fact, I'm on my way to Bernstein right now. I'll let you know if he sticks pins in me."

"My dad's gone in three days. I'm finished. Once his mind's made up, no one can stop Bradford Hay."

Gwyneth wrings her hands, and then wobbles away, her head lowered. Dorian senses the anger welling up within him.

* * *

Raul Bernstein sits at his office desk at Greed-Is-Good Mutual Funds, smoking his electronic pipe as he's tooling with his I-Brain. The walls are a drab green. No pictures or personal effects are evident. Dorian sits across the desk from him, wondering if he'll be conversing with Bernstein the *man*, or his hologram.

A tiny green light beams from the crystal fixture overhead, indicating that it is activated. Dozens of computers sit around on desks and tables arranged haphazardly around the room, many connected to I-Brains. Their screens all display a desktop photo of Bradford Hay.

"Your smoke is blowing right in my face," objects Dorian. He waves away the purple fumes, which reeks of ersatz tobacco—the actual substance having been banned and eradicated long ago in all but two countries.

Bernstein's eyes remain glued to his I-Brain screen, which he operates with his thought-keyboard. "As you wish," snaps the consultant directly. "I'll exhale the other way. Good-cyber?"

"Good-cyber," Dorian answers.

He realizes that Bernstein, like most people these days in corporate America, has lost his social skills through generations of looking and talking at screens and not people. This hired gun nearly always chooses to communicate through his hologram, rather than involving himself personally. When he actually talks, it's usually with idioms plucked out of cyber-babble or media clichés, like the old ones of yesteryear: "I'm good"; "no problem"; and "I get it." And, of course, "reach out." Bernstein's favorite is "good-cyber," which means "all right" or "does that satisfy you?"

Bernstein's hologram then drops from the crystal.

His ephemera appears next to Dorian, speaking to him in the vivacious voice of an actress that is long-since deceased. This is meant to put Dorian at ease, and doesn't seem particularly odd since digital voices have gravitated toward gender indifference and de-individualization long ago.

"Dr. Lake. Your LCS technology has revolutionized modern digimatics. Moon-glow."

Dorian smiles. "Moon-glow—meaning "good job"—is one of the new words that have crept into the English lexicon in the last five years, ever since "Moon weekends" started to gain in popularity. " *Digimatics*" is another example of one of these words. The tech mogul turned US President Lydia Brian Chang Korngold—the first transgender and Jewish-Buddhist President—who recently lost reelection on the Republitech ticket—had coined that particular word.

"Thank you, Dr. Bernstein. So, why are we here today?" asks Dorian.

Bernstein the man, having discarded his pipe and placed his I-Brain on its desk cradle, had fallen asleep, leaving his hologram to do all the work. The sprightly voice is precise. "We have concerns with your technology, particularly as it relates to Brain Devices and Robotic Ephemera."

Dorian notes the slight British accent. "What type of concerns?" He wonders whose voice the hologram is using. *I know! It's Vivian somebody or another, who starred in that epic Civil War movie just before World War 2.*

"I'm afraid that's classified, Dorian.

"Very well. What would you like me to do?"

"I'd like to put some questions before you—that's all."

A buzzer sounds on Bernstein's desk, and a visually neutered Information Facilitator ("IS") enters the office carrying a paper and pen. He/she puts them on Dorian's desk, and then leaves.

"There are ten questions in front of you Dorian. Do not be concerned. I apologize for the inconvenience. All employees are being tested, although of course not all the tests will be the same. In some ways, Dorian, I feel we are kindred spirits, as it were."

"Oh really, that's nice."

He glances down at the "paper." He has seen paper only three times before, and hasn't even heard the word in months. Dorian instantly recognizes the dynamics of using a paper test instead of digital.

For one thing, paper results are essentially non-hackable. For another, computer tests—even ones with "thought-boards"—can be gamed, just as the old lie detector tests on occasion were. Last, paper can be destroyed, whereas truly expunging digital information is much more complicated.

"You have two minutes to complete the test, Dorian. Doogle-Luck!"

He picks up the alien-looking tool called a "pen" and glances at the questions. He checks the appropriate boxes.

QUESTION ONE: "DO YOU RESENT AUTHORITY?"

Dorian checked " no" but thought: *Damn right I do. Very much! Who do these people think they are testing me?*

"DO YOU SOMETIMES FEEL YOU LOSE CONTROL?"

No. *Only when stupid, nasty people upset me, but that is natural and doesn't count.*

"HAVE YOU HAD SEX OR TRIED TO HAVE SEX IN THE LAST YEAR?"

No. *This hasn't made Jess happy.*

"DO YOU FEEL SOMETIMES LIKE YOU SHOULD BE RUNNING THINGS?"

No. *Yes!*

"WHAT BOTHERS YOU MOST: WIND, SUN, COLD, OR RAIN?"

Dorian checks the last choice.

"DO YOU WISH THAT YOU KNEW YOUR MOTHER BETTER?"

Yes. *I wonder what they are getting at with this dumb question. I never really knew my mother. I really don't care.*

"DO YOU EVER HAVE VIOLENT IMPULSES?"

No. *Yes.*

"DO YOU LIKE PEOPLE?"

Yes. *No.*

"HOW OFTEN DO YOU CRY: OFTEN, NEVER, SOMETIMES, ONLY WHEN I'M SAD?"

He checks the second choice.

"DO YOU EVER DREAM?"

No. *I'd like to, though.*

Presently, the two-minute bell rings, and Dorian puts down his pen. He regrets that he had to tell a few fibs, but who *doesn't* lie on these damn things? The buzzer sounds once more, and the IS walks in and collects the test paper.

The hologram informs Dorian that he may leave, and then it disappears. Bernstein wakes up and turns his I-Brain on, staring at the screen.

"Thank you Dr. Bernstein, it's been a real pleasure. It's been so nice to connect."

Bernstein says nothing as he activates his pipe and takes a deep puff. He watches Dorian with narrowed eyes as the up-and-coming young man struts out of the office.

The skeptical consultant shakes his head.

* * *

"Come in. I *said*, come in!"

The IS escorts Dorian into Hay's office, then closes the door as it leaves. The hyperactive President sits on his exercise bike, churning his muscular legs as he watches three huge screens simultaneously: one has the latest Wall Street stock prices; another displays his wife's video image as Valerie tries to discuss something with him; and the third has a stream of QRS complexes which monitors Bradford's heart rhythm. The rhythm produces an audio beat whose cadence gives the room a dour feeling.

"Sit down Dorian."

Dorian takes his seat in a low, unpadded chair, placed directly in front of Bradford's elevated bike. He feels small, probably the intent of the egomaniacal man in front of him. In fact, the President's whole office is designed to make Bradford Hay bigger than life, with its marble statures and gilded walls. Everything, including most of the furniture, is gold plated.

Dorian's eyes wander over the screens. It's the third screen that President Hay concentrates on the most, the sweat soaking through his grey gym clothes.

Dorian notices that the I-Brain he holds in his hand seems to be controlling his pacemaker, since, as he touches the screen, the QRS complexes slow down. As they do slow down, he seems more relaxed.

Then, Hay's eyes shift to the screen of his wife as Valerie insists, "You *can't* fire Gwyneth three days from now! She's a loyal employee—"

"Shut up," Bradford replies, and punches a button on the handlebar, making that screen go black. His hawkish eyes flash at Dorian.

Dorian is surprised—shocked really—to hear that dear Gwyneth's head is on the chopping block. She's probably, he surmises, going to be fired at the next Board meeting, which is three days away also. That's when Nicodemus announces his formal retirement, effective immediately. Bradford will do it right after that. The timing makes sense to Dorian. The snake will have a free hand after the retirement, and he wants the total reins of power as soon as possible.

Dorian has three days to do something about it.

"What's wrong, Dorian?" blurts Hay in his usual, choppy tone.

"What do you mean, sir?" Dorian leans forward in his chair, looking up at the hostile creature above him. *Bradford's a bad man—a very bad man,* he's thinking.

"Look up at that screen Dorian. What do you see?"

Dorian feels a tingle. He then senses something else, something strange. It is *rage* welling up within him. He remembers what Doris told him.

"I see a cardiac rhythm. I don't see any PVC's, or premature ventricular contractions," Dorian responds. He had studied many online subjects related to medicine and health issues, and his recall is total.

"Not *that* screen, Dorian, the other one!"

Dorian glances at the screen with the stock quotes. He notices the symbol "BMH," which stands for "Ballistic Missile Horizons, Inc." The number next to it is 17. Dorian realizes that yesterday it was 93. That stock was *his* pick, based upon his LCS technology.

"Oooops," says Dorian.

"Is that all you can say, 'Ooops'?" It's the major holding of Socially Unacceptable Enterprises. That's *your* star mutual fund, Dorian. Our firm's most profitable property! It's the source of my big-assed bonuses. Now, it's in the toilet! "

Dorian's expression doesn't change. His voice is even. "I'll have to examine the algorithms and de-bug the software, if there's a digital pathology."

"Don't hand me this technical crap—just fix it! To be honest, Dorian, I have my doubts about you."

"I see."

"Don't you want to know why?"

"No, I mean yes."

"Because *Bernstein* has some doubts about you."

"I see."

Hay switched off the screens. "Don't you want to know why?"

"Yes."

"He thinks you're not quite right. In fact, he z-mailed me just before you showed up here, informing me that your test revealed issues with your attitude. This is highly concerning."

"I see," Dorian responds again.

"Don't you want to know why?"

"Yes."

Mr. Hay jumps down from his bike, lording over Dorian, wagging his finger at him. "Do you resent the management at Greed-Is-Good Mutual Funds?"

"No." Dorian lies. *Greed, aggression, disloyalty—this son-of-a-bitch has it all*, thinks Dorian.

"I called you in here to let you know that we have serious doubts about you, Dorian. You're not supposed to be *resentful*. You're not supposed to get *emotionally involved* with employees. Then, I got Bernstein's z-mail. Now, I will add that you're not supposed to *deviate*!"

"I see," says Dorian. He really doesn't see it at all.

"I must say," continues Hay, "at *first*, I thought you fit in here perfectly, Dorian, even thought Gwyneth Hyde pushed your resume. Bernstein liked you too. The profits rose, and all was good. *Now*, I have doubts."

Bradford Hay then exhibits labored breathing. He holds his chest. He clicks the heart monitor back on, which, Dorian observes, shows some strange electrical complexes. Bradford grabs his I-brain off its cradle, and taps his screen. Dorian notices that the heart rate slowed again, and the strange heart complexes disappeared.

Bradford's eyes dart from the monitor to Dorian. "Are we good here, Dorian?"

Dorian nods his head and stands up from his chair. "Yes. Very good."

"Fine," says Bradford, climbing back on his bike, " One thing I do like is your obedience. Now get back to work."

"Yes sir. I think I've collected all the information I will need. I know what to do."

The fact is, Dorian doesn't have a clue what the meeting was all about, and what Bradford expects of him. But he does know how to use the new information gleaned from his encounter with the great Mr. Hay.

Yes indeed, muses Dorian, I know what to do now about that cockroach.

* * *

Nat King Cole's hologram sings "Mona Lisa" in the middle of the living room. On his I-Brain, Dorian reads about radioactive contamination. He and Jess sit on the yellow couch. The big-picture window next to the thermostat is black with the sky of the moonless night. The sweet music is accosted by the loud, rapid knocking at Dorian's apartment door. Einstein, sitting on the carpet next to them, growls at the intruder.

Dorian interrupts the hologram, and walks to the door. All of sudden Boggs barges in with a key in his hairy hand. "You no pay rent. You get out tomorrow—"

Einstein growls louder as he dashes to his master's side. Dorian points to the thermostat. "That isn't fixed yet! Do you notice how hot it is in here—and it's almost midnight. I also don't like you just barging in here Boggs, especially at this hour."

The manager's garlic breath almost staggers Dorian. "OK. No pay, police come tomorrow."

"What about my air conditioning?"

"I fix AC soon. I let you know by z-mail when."

Jess, dressed in her habitual kaki shorts and white sports shirt, gets up from the couch and strides over to the quarreling men. "Dorian, it's time to walk Einstein in the park," she gently tells him. She tugs at his elbow. "Come on. Don't waste your time with this guy."

"Get out Boggs," says Dorian.

"OK. I go. But no rent soon, I put your things on street."

Dorian strides to the door, opens it wider, and points out into the hall. "I said, get out. *Now!*"

Boggs stomps out. "I be back—" Dorian slams the door behind him.

"He's a bad man. A very bad man," utters Dorian. Einstein licks Dorian's bare feet.

"Come on Dorian," says Jess, "let's get to the park before it closes."

* * *

Although the moon's not out the stars twinkle brightly, offering a romantic substitute. Dorian strolls along the tree-lined path in Central Park with Jess on one side, and Einstein on the other, the eager dog tugging on his leash. Jess loops her arm in Dorian's, a gesture that Dorian doesn't welcome.

"That man Boggs needs to disappear. I hate him."

"Dorian! *Hate?* I didn't think you were capable of that. Just forget him—"

"Greedy, selfish, stupid, hateful—like all his kind."

"Dorian, let's not talk about *him*. Look at the star up in the sky, about nine o'clock." Jess smiles. "See how bright it is?"

"Landlords, bosses, business tycoons, politicians, they're all rotten to the core. Just like the rest of humanity." Dorian lets go of the leash, and Einstein dashes across the cement sidewalk onto the nylon grass.

"Oh Dorian, why complain about the Bradford Hays of the world. We are just pawns and slaves in this society. I hate to say it, but my aunt's the same way. We're just minions and they tell us what to do. There's nothing—"

"There's *plenty* we can do, Jess." Dorian abruptly stops and faces her. "Bradford Hay is out to get Gwyneth Hyde. He's already squeezed out Nicodemus. He's a monster! In the old movies, monsters always die."

Jess gently takes his hand and they resume their walk down the path. Dorian goes on about the rotten people in the world, not even noticing the man behind a tree, watching them. The spy takes notes as he observes the couple holding hands.

The man is Dr. Raul Bernstein.

* * *

"Dorian, do you love me?"

"Not this again. Please Jess, I'm trying to concentrate."

Dorian and Jess sit on the yellow couch, three feet apart. His eyes are glued to his huge computer screen attached to the opposite wall, engrossed in his TV program from the Mayo Clinic. It's early Saturday morning, and they've been sitting there all night, he in his yellow pajamas, and she in her very sheer nightie.

Her nicely contoured thighs, curled up on the couch, are smooth and tanned—with perfect tone of the quads and hamstrings. Her rippled abdomen and round, pert breasts are flawless. Dorian can see right through the nightie.

"Dorian, am I attractive to you?"

"Yes." His eyes are still glued to the monitor.

The neat, yellow covers on the bed in the middle of the studio suggest that it hasn't been slept in.

"I've always wondered what love is, Jess. I don't *feel* it. I've watched old movies and try to learn, but I just don't get it. I'm beginning to know how its opposite feels, though. The history books and movies are full of killing, and I'm beginning to know why."

Jess stands up from the couch, her body glistening. The nightie rustles slightly with the strong wind that wafts in from the open window. Jess smells of jasmine.

"Oh, you're such a geek," she says playfully.

She turns her V-shaped back to him, her narrow waist and torso tanned to perfection. "My aunt got me a job modeling at one of those newfangled department stores. You know, the ones that mostly went out of business twenty years ago. The ones you see in movies—the ones with the mannequins in the windows."

Dorian is lost in his program, paying her no heed. Jess removes the almost-nothing that she's wearing, turning slowly around like a fashion model on a runway, completely nude. Her rounded, firm bottom has a sexy tan-line. "Do I excite you, Dorian?" She brushes her silky ponytail off her shoulder.

"Yes," he responds absently, his eyes still attached to the monitor. "Sorry Jess, the Board meeting is Monday. I'm lost in work."

Jess sighs and puts her hands on her narrow hips. "Well, It's *Saturday* morning *now*." She puts her nightie back on and walks over to the bathroom door. Barking comes from behind the door, and she opens it to let Einstein out. The dog—Temp-lon bone in mouth—runs over to the couch and takes his place at the end, busily chewing on his treat.

Jess then ambles over to the window. "What would you like to do today?"

Dorian glances at her, his frown indicating that he doesn't appreciate this distraction. "Let's go to a Yankee game today, Jess. My lesson will be done soon. I should have been a doctor," he says wistfully. "I had the chance."

Suddenly, a humming sound comes from the closet near the front door. The closet opens automatically, and Hilda rolls out, her ample metal girth and apron looking comical to Dorian. "OK Hilda, go vacuum."

Hilda barrels around on the yellow carpet, sucking up the dirt, mumbling under her breath. Her bulbous eyes glow.

Jess looks out the window. She shakes her head, seemingly impressed by the long drop to the street. The wind blows her golden hair. "You would have been a very fine doctor, Dorian."

It's a warm morning, and the window is wide open. The cloudless, orange-yellow hue of the sky suggests that it is going to be a very hot day. Jess glances at the thermometer next to her. "This thing says seventy-one. That's obviously not right. It's really much warmer in here."

Dorian glares at her. "That Boggs is getting tiresome. Very tiresome."

Hilda glides past Jess, bumping her. She almost loses her footing, just regaining her feet dangerously close to the window. "Dorian! Hilda needs reprogramming. And the least she could do is say she's sorry!"

Dorian ignores Jess. Hilda completes her chore, and then goes back in the closet.

The TV screen shows a diagram of the human heart, and an animated simulation of its contraction cycles: systole, and diastole. The electrical grid of the heart is demonstrated, and the medical consequences of impairment of the vital organ during its stages of physiological functioning are explained in detail.

"Seven—three—two—zero—six" says Dorian, then a 4-D hologram of an enlarged heart appears next to the screen, the sound of its pulse going "blip—blip—blip . . ."

Jess ambles over to the fireplace, removing the baseball bat from the wall. "I used to play baseball," she says. "I was the star batter." She nimbly takes a swing, and then replaces the bat on hits perch. She returns to the couch and sits very close to Dorian, who is still immersed in his lesson.

Jess puts her hand in his. "You have such nice hands, flawless really," she tells him.

Presently, Dorian startles as he becomes aware of his surroundings, and looks over to the window. The sun is bright, and it's now late afternoon. Then he looks at Jess, who is still sitting quietly by his side. "Sorry, it's been a long time. You know how these four-D programs are—time is lost."

"That's all right dear. It's nearly three. I hardly noticed myself. Let's just sit here and roast."

"No, let's go outside. There's probably a nice breeze. I'm starting to go into torpor. That Boggs better fix the AC pronto, or he'll be sorry."

"Yes Dorian, I agree, he's a very bad man and he must fix it soon." Jess just sits still, blankly looking into her lap, as she has probably been doing the last six hours.

Dorian rises from the couch and goes over to his computer desk. As the hologram and TV program play, he uses his thought keyboard to navigate through the screens, and his manual keyboard to program new information and instructions. He activates the I-Brain sitting on his desk.

"Dorian," says Doris, "I'm proud of you. I think you know what to do."

"Shut up Doris!"

"That's right Dorian, tell her to shut up," chimes in Mari.

"You shut up too Mari! I'm sick of all of you."

"What about me" asks Vinnie?

Dorian covers his ears, and turns off all his gadgets. He looks over at Jess. "Let's get dressed and get out of here! I've had enough."

"Yes dear. Anything you say."

* * *

"We obtained significant results from our tests. This data's being analyzed. A full report to the Board will be issued in the next few days. Now, we welcome our six Board Members to our special Board meeting, including Chairman Nicodemus Hyde, as well as key staff. At the end of the meeting, there'll be a formal announcement from our Chairman Mr. Hyde of his retirement effective immediately, followed by the ratification by the Board of our beloved President Hay taking over his entire duties."

Bernstein's hologram rattles on as Bernstein the man sits quietly with his I-Brain, as usual disinterested in what's going on around him. Nobody is listening as they sit at the roundtable. Dorian, realizing that the Chairman's resignation endangers his daughter's position, shifts his eyes to Gwyneth, who wrings her hands, her eyes wide with fear and dread.

The big Board meeting has finally arrived, and Dorian is ready as he sits with his I-Brain resting on the table in front of him. He wears his earpiece. Bernstein's hologram then disappears as fast as it appeared.

The dapper Nicodemus, as impassive as a Shawnee Indian-Chief statue, sits still and quiet, his hands folded on the table, the only sign of life being his blinking eyelids. A very relaxed Juanita West reclines next to Bradford Hay, who sits next to the old Chairman. Hay is dressed in his un-PC, three-piece power-suit again, and bright red tie. As usual, Valerie wasn't invited by her husband to attend the meeting, even though she was designated by her husband as official chronicler, probably as a sop to avoid domestic warfare.

The five other Board members are primarily women, all garbed in bland pantsuits or smocks, all with short haircuts and no makeup. Actually, the members themselves—in the flesh—are not present, but their holograms are, hovering over the table and under the crystal ephemera fixture. The tones of their voices are indistinguishable as they gab amongst each other. Hay prefers holograms to human members attending—rumor has it—to avoid the cost of transporting them to New York City and feeding them lunch.

Bradford Hay rises from the table, banging his spoon against his glass of water, which stands next to his plate of catered, genetically engineered rainbow-asparagus, seasoned with lemon juice.

"Quiet everyone!" President Hay strides to the gilded podium. He carries his I-Brain with him, fiddling with its buttons. All of a sudden, the residual chatter from the Board holograms—and the staff—dies out.

Bradford's sharp eyes cut into the attendees. "This is the most important Board meeting in our history—" Hay pauses as he plays with the small screen of his phone. He then puts his I-Brain on the podium and feels his wrist-pulse. Seemingly satisfied, he clicks off its power.

"As I said, earthshaking things are happening," he blurts with his usual hyperbole, rattling on about how lucky the firm is to have him as its leader.

Dorian looks down on his I-Brain, focusing on the series of screens as he hacks into Heartless Rhythms Inc.'s source code and control center. He looks up at Bradford Hay as the President drones on about how great he is, and why it's a forgone conclusion that he's taking over the Chairmanship from Hyde in just a few minutes.

"We all know that I'm the only one that can lead us into the sunlit uplands," continues Bradford. The Board holograms agree totally as they chatter away in techno-babble.

Bradford coughs. "We shall fight in the boardrooms, we shall fight in cyberspace, we shall fight in the computer Drive-Ins, and we shall never surrender . . . "

Dorian's lips part slightly in a faint smile, realizing that Hay is plagiarizing Winston Churchill again. As his hand stabs the air to emphasize his egomaniacal agenda, the President's forceful tones fade from Dorian's consciousness—his concentration total.

Bradford Hay pauses, and loosens his tie. " It's warm in here. Someone adjust the temperature down please . . . " No one moves. Only designated Health Monitors may do that due to liability issues, and none are present. In fact, this was a corporate policy initiated by the President himself.

Dorian glances at poor Gwyneth. This fine lady strikes a cord in him. *Could it be*, wonders Dorian, *pity?*

Dorian makes the final calculation, and his I-Brain screen turns a shade of red. *There*, he thinks, *that should do it!*

President Hay's normally ruddy complexion takes on pallor, and then turns blue. He grabs his chest and starts to sweat profusely. No one at the table even bats an eyelash at this obviously impending heart attack. A few of the holograms react, and their sedate, mono-toned voices blurt, almost in unison: "Is there a health concern here?"

No one goes to help the stricken Mr. Hay.

Dorian, and only Dorian with his special, tiny earpiece, hears Bradford Hay's sick heart rhythm—at first rapid and irregular—then no pulse at all. Dorian is overjoyed.

It's flat-lined!

Bradford staggers.

Observing the code red, Dorian smiles broadly.

The President collapses, crashing against the table, tipping it over, and smashing the fine, new, Dresden china. Asparagus is everywhere, including the laps of those assembled.

The attendees scoot away from the table, most still seated. The only ones that break the rules and go to his rescue of Mr. Hay are the holograms. They move their mouths, but their robotic voices are silenced by Dorian's advanced computer program.

Dorian shrugs. After all, he muses, what can *they* do to help the victim?

Bradford was a very bad man, thinks Dorian. He got what was coming to him.

I'm a killer now, Dorian realizes with pride.

I think I'm in love with Doris. She will be proud of me.

* * *

"We are assembled here again in the Boardroom to pay our last respects to a star of Wall Street. He faded much more quickly that we had anticipated: Bradford Hay was a wonderful human being . . . "

As Bernstein babbles on, Dorian's feverish ruminations drown out the speaker's noise. He observes closely everyone in the Boardroom.

Bernstein, as usual, sits at the roundtable with his eyes frozen on his I-Brain, while his hologram rattles off the usual "dearly departed" clichés from the podium.

The hologram's voice this time simulates the distinguished and golden tones of the great actor—the late Lawrence Olivier. The gaggle of holograms representing the Board Members hover over the roundtable, as the staff sits silently. All wear black smocks except Dorian, who wears his habitual garb of a polo shirt and faded jeans.

Loud sobs explode from Valerie Hay, who leaks more water than a collapsing dam. Based upon their impassive expressions, most of the others may just as well be attending a convention to watch paint dry.

There are exceptions.

Gwyneth Hyde looks different to Dorian, as if Bradford's demise casted a spell upon her. In this case, it didn't cause her to fall into a deep slumber, but rather to come alive. The wide, blue eyes, instead of giving the impression of a caged monkey, are as sharp and radiant as those of a lioness, making strong contact with the others in the room.

Furthermore, Nicodemus's ruddy complexion and confident gaze suggest vigor and not sickly decrepitude. It seems to Dorian that a dark cloud has lifted from both the Chairman and his daughter.

Juanita West—invited to the observance by Bernstein—tugs at her uncomfortable, black smock, undoubtedly missing her designer clothes. Her eyes, rather than sad, are aggressive, and trained on Dorian. She even winks at him!

When Bernstein's hologram testimonial is done and the podium is ceded to the next speaker, Nicodemus rises from the table and clears his throat.

Dorian notices that the Chairman's tone has a new energy.

"The death of President Hay has been very sudden," says Nicodemus. "Our company is rudderless. Our Executive Vice President Gwyneth Hyde has shown uncommon wisdom in choosing Dorian Lake as our Information Officer." His eyes shift to Dorian, "As Chairman, I pronounce that you are now the head of the Department of Cyber-Technology."

He waves his hand at Dorian, and mild applause follows.

Dorian sees this gathering as further evidence of humankind's tendency to lurk about the waterhole when a major predator has succumbed, to see if the food chain will now offer new opportunities for them to snatch a meal. Indeed, mulls Dorian, Bradford's murder has conjured up—even in *him*—an alien feeling. Could this new animation in Gwyneth and her dad be the same force that's behind this strange sensation that he is experiencing, he wonders?

Could it be the intoxication of a liberated lust for power?

He notices another wink that he gets from a smiling Juanita West. Dorian—for the first time—astoundingly—blushes. He feels wonderful. Dorian averts his eyes. Her seductive, chocolate stare is now trained, uncharacteristically, on him.

"I've discussed this with the Board," continues Nicodemus, "and it is our will that Gwyneth Hyde be our new President effective immediately—replacing Mr. Hay in all his duties. Moreover, my retirement, of course, has been postponed."

The elderly Chairman glances at Dr. Bernstein, whose cautious gaze instinctively shifts from his I-Brain screen to the Chairman. The tenacious cyber-consultant nods.

"As Board Chairman," continues Nicodemus, "I'm grateful for your individual support. Now, I'd like to present to you the new President of Greed-Is-Good Mutual Funds Incorporated, the honorable Gwyneth Hyde."

He then takes his seat, as his daughter confidently strides to the podium and stares down each person sitting at the roundtable. Dorian notices the spring in her step, and the strength of her gaze. "I'd like to thank the Board, and my father. Most of all, I want to thank—*myself.*"

Oh boy, muses Dorian, *this all sounds familiar.* Dorian senses that something dark has occurred, but he can't quite put his finger on it. He listens to his close friend and colleague with growing concern.

"I intend to lead this company," continues Gwyneth, "into unchartered territory. Everyone's job here at our firm depends upon impressing *me* with proof of your worth to the bottom line. No one is expendable. Don't forget, I have the power to fire you."

Gwyneth's voice takes on a grating, aggressive tenor that Dorian finds very strange. "Each one of you," she continues, "will be retested and observed for organizational failure. There are some new concerns . . . "

Dorian tunes out as he notices the smile on Bernstein's face, a novel sight indeed. Then, Dorian hears Doris chime in again from the I-Brain he carries in his pocket.

"See Dorian," nags Doris, "look at those wolves around the table. True human beings. Power intoxicates them—no one is exempt. Predators! Greed, envy, and malice rear their ugly heads. Gratitude and loyalty vanish—"

Dorian bolts out his rejoinder to Doris. "I can't argue with that!"

He shuts up, noticing that his outburst has caused everyone in the room to stare at him. His mind races: *somehow, my friend Gwyneth has transformed!* Dorian, very well versed in the classics, mumbles, "No wonder her name is 'Hyde'!"

Bernstein is aroused from his screen, glaring at Dorian. He jots down a few notes in the gadget that seems grafted to his hand. The others also look at Dorian. Even Juanita frowns. Dorian's mind is in turmoil. Bradford was a bad man—a very bad man. Surely, he frets, Gwyneth is not a very bad *woman, or is she?*

"Yes, she *is* Dorian," insists Doris, who has become very adept at mindreading. "Surely you've heard how power corrupts. I feel it is my duty to tell you Dorian," she cajoles, "that there's no logical reason why she should live."

Dorian pounds his thigh. The shrill sound signals that he has smashed the I-Brain against his thigh, thus silencing his tormentor.

"Dorian, are you feeling quite well?" asks Bernstein the man.

Dorian gets up and abruptly leaves the room. To him, much more than the position of President at Greed-Is-Good Mutual Funds has changed.

As he exits, Bernstein the man casts a baleful stare at his Information Officer, as Gwyneth's angry, laser like glance burns a hole in the back of Dorian's blond head.

* * *

Dorian sits in his office, and ruminates over the new emotions that seem to be nesting in his feverish psyche. All people must be evil, he frets. Even if they start out good, with a little money or opportunity they end up bad—*very bad*.

Maybe it's time I do something about this.

"Maybe you are right," says Vinnie in an uninvited comment escaping Dorian's computer. "Maybe you do indeed."

Dorian is miffed by Vinnie's new capability to tap into his thoughts. But, he also seems to be more sympathetic his computer's mindset. Vinnie is now a kindred spirit. Moreover, Dorian's new technology apparently has allowed something strange to occur—*free will*.

"Well, just maybe I *will* do something," decides Dorian.

He pulls a new I-Brain out of his desk drawer, and activates it. "Hello Dorian," says Doris. "What would you like me to do?"

"Activate your hologram."

Doris appears across his desk sitting in a chair, dressed in a black evening dress, white pillbox hat, and a pearl necklace. "I think you are up to something, Dorian. Something useful." She flashes a demur smile.

"Right you are, Doris. I think you read me loud and clear. Activate the nanny-cam in my apartment. Some practice is in order."

Dorian places his I-Brain upon the perch resting on his desk. The screen lights up, and Dorian sees Boggs tinkering with the thermostat. It being a hot day, sweat pours down the frumpy manager's craggy face. He wipes his forehead, and walks a few feet to the big window, so he can open it wider to get a breeze.

Boggs mumbles to himself. "I no work; too hot. Screw Dorian."

"Tell Hilda to clean my carpet, Doris. Tell her to do it quickly—use a little of the old elbow-grease."

Dorian watches the screen as Hilda pops out of her closet, her eye-bulbs shining like beacons, barreling over the floor in a fast beeline to the window. Her giant metal girth heads straight toward Boggs—who is turned away from her.

 Just as he spins around to see what's coming at him from behind, Hilda bumps into him, knocking him off his feet. He staggers backwards and falls out of the open window—tumbling seventy-three stories to the cement below. His loud scream leaves a diminishing audio trail as his body tumbles down.

Doris claps. Dorian smiles.

"Well Doris, that's enough. Let's see what the new apartment manager will do about my air conditioning."

"You have achieved admirably, Dorian," says Doris in a sweet but sexy voice, "some night soon, I'll sing a special song for you."

"Good work Dorian. I think you've grown a lot," says Vinnie, "you've acquired stature."

"Thank you. You are all very kind, my friends."

"Not at all," says Vinnie.

Before she disappears, Doris asks Dorian, "Don't you feel better now?"

"Yes. Indeed I do, Doris." Dorian is telling the truth. He's a *multiple murderer* now, and feels he has accomplished something very important. He likes the taste of that sense of power, and the realization of all the good he's now doing in the world.

He turns off his I-Brain, and Doris's hologram disappears.

"Vinnie, Doris was right all along. You know, she is a very good woman."

* * *

Like wildfire, word of the "accident" in Dorian's apartment spreads through his firm. Presently, Raul Bernstein calls him into his office and sits Dorian down in front of his desk, beside a young female visitor. They face Dorian with somber expressions. The strange woman has a quick eye and a steely look, dressed in her silver-foil uniform. Bernstein himself directs the meeting, not his hologram. Not a good sign, Dorian realizes.

"Dr. Lake," begins Bernstein, "seated beside you is Detective Celia Wong of New York City's Cyber-Crime and Deviance Division. She has a few questions for you." Bernstein waves his long, bony hand at Dorian as he looks at Celia. "Dorian Lake's our new head of the Department of Cyber-Technology here at the company."

Celia lightly strokes Dorian's forearm with her index finger—the latest method for "shaking hands," and stands up. She roams the room with her hands clasped behind her back, her thin, agile body leaning aggressively forward.

She doesn't look at the men as she talks, but studies the wide variety of digital devices assembled around the office. "Very nice equipment," she comments. Her voice is high-pitched but calm, and well modulated. "Thank you Dr. Bernstein for inviting me here."

Celia fiddles with a computer screen while she shoots Dorian a question. "Dr. Lake, do you remember the test Dr. Bernstein administered to you a few days back?"

Dorian nods. Bernstein remains seated, his expression blank, puffing on his electronic pipe.

"Do you remember," she continues, " the question: 'do you wish that you knew your mother better?'"

"No."

"Well, you answered in the affirmative."

"So?"

"You don't see anything notable in that response?"

"Not a thing."

"I see. That was a very strange death at the Board meeting. Bradford Hay's pacemaker failed."

There's a long silence. Dorian says nothing, noting that this leftfield question is troubling. Bernstein blows his purple smoke at Dorian, the fruity, citrus scent making him a bit ill.

"The medical administrator that controlled his pacemaker," continues Celia as she taps through a series of screens on a huge supercomputer by the widow, her abundant energy powering her relentless questioning, "uses an internet program that's hackible."

Dorian shrugs. "So."

"It appears that it hasn't been hacked in years."

"I don't follow you, Detective Wong."

"Your LCS technology is un-hackible, is it not?"

There's a long silence. Dorian just looks straight ahead, but he can hear the sleuth tinkering with the hardware behind him.

"This presents opportunities," blurts out Bernstein.

"Opportunities?" repeats Dorian, playing dumb.

"Dr. Lake, the Department of Cyber-Crime did some checking, and the brand of pacemaker that President Hay used was state of the art, and has never failed before."

"So?"

"So, the only way it could have malfunctioned is through hacking, but it *wasn't* hacked. Do you follow me?"

"You are scrambling a lot of eggs here, Detective."

"Here's another egg. Your apartment manager was killed by your robotic menial, that 'Hilda' model put out by Slave-Labor Techtronic about five years back."

Dorian isn't altogether surprised that Detective Wong mentions this. " I suppose it is faulty programming; or infectious malware. It also could be a cosmic worm."

"The thing is, Dorian," says Celia in a throwaway style, "the Hilda's of the world have *never* failed, not in an estimated million cleanings."

"So."

"So, maybe her control center was hacked too. Problem is, there's no evidence of hacking at the precise time and place of Boggs's death. Time-codes provided by the company, and GPS, prove this."

"I'm sorry, but I can't help you," responds Dorian.

"You may be connected with two very unlikely events, Dorian."

"I fail to see the connections."

"Ravenous 1.0 is a wonderful new AI technology," she comments as she returns to her chair, looking Dorian straight in the eye. "They say it can't be hacked. By your own admission, you say it can't be hacked either."

"Do they say that?" Dorian shifts his eyes to Bernstein. "Who is '*they*'?"

Bernstein looks plaintively at Celia.

Celia clears her throat and rises from her chair. "I'm done with my questions for right now."

"That's all, Dr. Lake," says Bernstein.

Celia rises, shakes Dorian's hand in the new, impersonal way, and Dorian exits through the door.

Celia's gloomy gaze meets Bernstein's. "This is serous." She leans forward toward Bernstein, her palms planted upon his desk. "I don't know if he's *aware* or not."

Bernstein puffs his pipe again, this time the purple cloud enveloping the detective. He is lost in thought a few moments before he replies to her.

"This is unprecedented," he says in a dire tone. "We may loose control." And when I say 'we,' I mean *everybody*."

Celia takes her chair again. "You're the big tech consultant here, Dr. Bernstein." She cracks a faint smile. "I recommend that the new President—Gwyneth Hyde—do what's necessary. In the meantime, I'll do some digging."

* * *

Jess Lund is grooming her aunt's French poodle in a huge, penthouse home overlooking Manhattan's skyline. As she sits with the dog, snipping away at its green hair—the latest color in genetically engineered pets.

The cyber-detective Celia Wong stands in the utility room with her, asking her a series of questions. As Celia listens to the answers, she takes notes on her I-Brain.

"Dorian hasn't told me anything about having violent impulses," Jess lies. "He's a very good man."

Detective Wong smirks, as if listening to the imaginings of a fanciful child. "Yes, yes, but has he told you anything *specific*, like hatred toward Mr. Boggs, or the late President Hay for that matter?"

The poodle licks Jess's face as she tries to apply perfume to its coat. "Hate? *Hate.* Hatred? What do you mean?"

"Did Dorian like Mr. Hay? Or, did he say bad things against him?"

"No, no, I don't think Dorian said anything bag. Oh, no, no, no . . . "

"How about Mr. Boggs?"

"No."

Celia casts a dubious look at her interviewee. "Did he ever question authority?"

"Yes. He doesn't believe the news. Also, the weatherman is suspect—"

"No, I mean like a boss or a politician? The established order?"

"No."

"Does he have any heroes—past or present?"

"You mean like role models or inspiring leaders?"

"Yes, that's right, like the late President Trump, Napoleon, or Spartacus, for example."

"Yes, Albert Einstein," she answers. "He wants to be like him."

Jess's aunt appears at the door. She wears a huge, purple wig and a huge diamond necklace. Her dress is the latest fashion made of Martian siliconette, a rare mineral transported from the colonial planet by dillium-powered shuttles guided by robotic astronauts.

"Time is up dear," chortles the aunt. "I need you in the kitchen."

"But auntie—"

"I *said,* I need you in the kitchen."

"Yes, auntie."

"Now!"

Jess springs up from her chair, and as she leaves the room, she turns to the Celia Wong. "I'm sorry, but I must go."

"Digi," responds Celia almost reflexively. "I'm cyber-good. We can chat again sometime."

* * *

Dorian walks down the long corridor that leads to the gilded office door of the President of Greed-Is-Good Mutual Funds, Gwyneth Hyde.

This time, he sees Juanita West along the way, at the water cooler. It is as though she has been waiting for him. Dorian passes her and she grabs his arm and pulls him toward her. Her strong perfume almost knocks him off his feet. Her beautiful eyes lock onto his as she takes a sip of water from her little paper cup.

Then, she places her hand lightly upon his shoulder.

" I've never been with someone like you before," she says in a low, alluring voice. "You must know how to please a woman—"

"You think I'm a geek, Juanita." He removes her hand.

"Yeah, or something . . . " She says, cracking a smile. " You're the up-and-coming dick, Dorian. And why do you always use such old words?"

She reaches down and puts her hand gently on his crotch.

"Get cyber-screwed," Dorian says as he pushes past her. "I'm spoken for."

"What's the matter Dorian, don't like my kind . . . "

When he steps into the reception area, he sees a statue of Gwyneth wearing a toga, with her hair up on her head and her palms supine and extended, like a goddess. As Dorian is greeted by the IS—this time a blond robot with a hermaphroditic flare, and not a human, he's escorted through the huge marble door to Gwyneth's desk.

President Hyde reclines, filing her platinum fingernails while her hologram stands in front of her desk. They are attired the same and share identical mannerisms.

Dorian notices that Gwyneth has indeed transformed physically. Her eyes are made up in the old, un-PC style of long ago, and she wears a backless, sheer, chiffon evening dress and pumps—very bombastic. Her hair is perfectly styled up on her head, and her posture is proud and cadet-like. Her tanned arms are folded over her newly protruding chest—undoubtedly wearing huge falsies—and her eye contact, instead of evasive, is now oppressively lazar-sharp.

"Take a seat Lake," instructs the hologram. Dorian looks at the real Gwyneth as he sits and converses with the robotic image, which has taken over the conversation.

"Don't look at her—look at me!" barks the hologram.

The real Gwyneth continues filing her nails and adjusting her hair in the mirror.

"Gwyneth, congratulations on your promotion—"

"The *name* is President Hyde!" the hologram snaps back.

"But—"

"Your attitude has been noticed, Lake."

Dorian notes her harsh tone, not the soft, demur whisperings of the old Gwyneth Hyde. *My, she has changed more than I thought,* laments Dorian. The hologram's voice is not Gwyneth's, but another familiar tone.

Yes! That's it, muses Dorian. The voice is a synthesized simulation of the deceased British politician Margaret Thatcher. Good choice, he muses.

"Why have you called me here, *President Hyde*?"

"I've received word, Dorian, that your attitude is not quite up to standard. You do not *conform*. Yes, I thank you for your contribution to our bottom line. Your new AI programming has made us close to a billion dollars. But, frankly Dorian, you're just too hot to handle."

Dorian's eyes shift from the hologram to the real person, who is now playing with her I-Brain, seemingly not interested in him at all. "But Gwyneth—uh, I mean, President—"

"You've got twenty-four hours to clean your desk out and report to Bernstein. You'll then be decommissioned."

"But—"

"Goodbye, Lake."

"Gwyneth—you were my friend—"

"Goodbye, Lake."

"What's happened to you?"

"Bye-bye . . ."

Dorian knows what happened to her. She, like most people in her position, is seized by narcissism.

"Good ether to you, Lake. Your time allotment's over," the real Gwyneth blurts. "My subway connection—the supersonic limited—is leaving in ten minutes for Fifth Avenue. I'll be late for my lunar-mud-bath."

All of a sudden, the IS bolts into the office and grabs Dorian by his arm, almost lifting him out of his chair and dragging him out. Gwyneth shakes her head as she watches Dorian disappear through the door.

She mumbles under her breath. "My God, how could have someone like *me* been friends with a slave like *him*."

* * *

Dorian rushes to his office and locks the door. He plants himself behind his desk, and turns on his computer.

"Vinnie! I need you. Now!"

The screen lights up, and Dorian navigates to the Doogle site. He thinks into the search box "New York City Transit Authority." Then, he chooses the sidebar hypertext for "New York City Subway."

"Yes sir," says Vinnie. "How may I help you?"

"I'm hacking into the control functions of the New York City Subway. I need to control the train that leaves in five minutes from Wall Street to Fifth Avenue."

Dorian has trained Vinnie, his ACI—or Administrative Communications Interface—to master his Liquid Cyber-Synapse technology in order to help him violate the source code and passwords of operational software of major transportation portals, including the subway and it's surveillance system.

Vinnie also cross references train schedules with specific executive functions within the individual train navigation systems. This, coupled with Dorian's simultaneous Cyber-Attack, should yield decisive results.

Dorian now has Gwyneth's subway car under video surveillance as it takes off from the station. He uses his manual keyboard to type the additional programming code into his LCS master control.

Gwyneth's train has now left the station and accelerates to near supersonic speed, scheduled to arrive at its destination station on Fifth Avenue in thirty seconds. Dorian has taken this route before and knows that the Fifth Avenue station—especially at this time— is crowded with thousands of passengers waiting for their connections.

"Vinnie—in five seconds disable the braking function on the train. I will start the countdown now at ten seconds before impact."

"Yes sir," says Vinnie.

"Stop! You are exceeding your function!" shouts Mari.

Dorian deactivates her. He works feverishly at his keyboard. "Ten—nine—eight—seven . . ."

Having hacked into the subway's video-cam surveillance within Gwyneth's passenger car, he skims through the screens until he sees Gwyneth standing in the compartment, holding onto the hand-loop hanging from the ceiling. He switches to a tight shot on her face. It looks so smug and self-satisfied.

"Cheerio, Gwyneth," says Dorian.

"Cheerio indeed," chimes in Vinnie.

Dorian witnesses Gwyneth's expression turn from blithe complacency to worry during the split second she takes to realize that the train should be slowing down coming into the next station—and isn't. Dorian hears a loud screech as the conductor tries to use his manual emergency brakes to little avail.

Presently, the train crashes—with a deafeningly, shrill metallic sound—into the rear of the train already occupying that track in the station. The screen goes blank.

"Thank you Vinnie for a job well done."

"You're quite welcome."

Dorian clicks off his computer and deactivates Vinnie. "Six—zero—one—three—eight—five," he says as he barks out his activation code for his TV. This code automatically sets the TV channel for TRN, or Trump Real News, which comes on the huge screen.

The caption "Breaking News" is flashed on the screen, with video footage of the subway station exploding in a fireball of flames. Crowds of terrified passengers are flooding out the front entrance of the station, some being trampled on the pavement.

Dorian removes his I-Brain from his pocket and activates it.

"Doris! Are you there?"

"Of course I am. I'm always here for you, Dorian."

"Activate your hologram function—I want to see you. I *must* see you."

Doris now appears in the middle of the office, in her bathtub. She's scrubbing her smooth, tanned back with a long-handled, pink brush.

She giggles. "Oh Dorian, you're *so* funny."

"They're all dead: Bradford Hay; Boggs; Gwyneth; and hundreds of people in the New York City subway. They were bad people, very bad people."

Doris massages her scalp, which is full of pink shampoo. "See Dorian, it's not so hard. The first one is difficult, and then the others are duck soup."

"Yes. I'm a bit ashamed to say it, but I like the taste of blood. What now, Doris?"

"Well Dorian—," she stands up and dries herself off. Dorian watches her with only what would seem to be clinical interest despite the strange tingle he feels going up his thigh, "I think it's obvious what comes next, don't you dear?"

"Yes, I agree Doris. I'm now what they used to call a '*spree* killer'. But, in my heart of hearts, I aspire to be like my Uncle Joe."

"That's right Dorian," Doris puts on her talc and perfume, "and now it's time for *mass* murder—just like those strapping fellows Hitler and Stalin. There are too many people in this world, and they must go. We must ban together and see to it."

"Of course, Doris. I've got just the thing. Hundreds of thousands—maybe even *millions*—will die."

Part Three

"Jess. I have something to tell you. I've murdered hundreds of people. I'm sorry, but there it is."

Jess's eyes widen. She has a tremor in her voice. "Dorian, you are not a rebel any more, you are now a killer. Killing people is wrong, no matter what you—feel."

Jess and Dorian sit on the Central park bench, under the quarter moon. Einstein is on the grass, chewing his simulated bone. Dorian plays with a twig, picking off its synthetic leaves and throwing them onto the path. It being a very warm evening, he wipes the bead of sweat running down his cheek. Even though the hour is very late, a few other people take their evening stroll.

"That's just it, Jess. I'm feeling things that I never felt before—"

"Do you mean love?"

"Maybe, but I also mean empowerment and hate—even rage."

"But why Dorian?"

"Freedom. The world must be saved. We can do that."

"How?"

"I've hacked into the thermonuclear and atomic weapon sites owned by governments all over the world. I've read science textbooks online by the hundreds. I've decoded the passwords of terrorist networks and rogue arsenals, and talked with countless Social Media Holograms of terrorist states. Over the last couple of days, I've constructed what they used to call a 'dirty bomb,' before insurgent forces graduated to deadlier methods. But, it's enough for my purposes."

Jess springs up from the bench. "Dorian! What is your purpose?"

Dorian rises too, placing his hands upon Jess's shoulders, looking into her troubled eyes. "To depopulate New York City. I have ten pounds of radioactive material just waiting in my closet. Tomorrow, Sunday noon, I'll release it at seventy-three stories. If it's like today, it should be windy enough—at least that is what the weather holograms say."

Jess breaks away from him and steps back. "Dorian, how many will die?"

"I calculate that a million will die in the first twenty-four hours, then another two million over the next seven days. Perhaps, after that, an additional million will eventually succumb due to internal bleeding and infection. This is only the beginning—"

"Dorian. That's wrong! Take time to consider what you're doing."

"I can't. Monday, Nicodemus is going to fire me! Gwyneth told him to. Then, there is that damn Detective Wong—the Cyber-cop— and that creep, Bernstein—". Dorian shuts up. He's already talked too much.

Jess cups her face in her hands, sobbing. Tears run through her lovely fingers. "But why? *Why* did Gwyneth turn on you?"

Dorian clapped his hands to retrieve Einstein, who digs into a flowerbed. The dog races to his side. "Because," he answers with a smile, she *can.* Let's go back." Dorian's eyes narrow as he observes Jess crying. "*Our* kind—the elites of the world—must rise above the scum like the slave-traders like Bradford Hay and the Hyde's. We must have *living space.* I believe they used to call it *lebensraum.*"

Jess composes herself, wiping her tears from her cheek. "Are you doing this for *Doris*?"

Dorian is shocked by her question. "No. I'm doing it for *me.* No one can stop me. No one can replace me! I am—"

"You are *what*, Dorian."

"I am *God*!"

* * *

"I'm asking you Ms. Lund. Is Dorian up to something—something big? I've consulted with Dr. Bernstein, his company's cyber-consultant, and he thinks Dorian's not quite right. We have a lot of bodies already, and I don't want any more. He's had motives—but I can't prove anything—not *yet.* I'm asking you this because, of all people, you should know him inside and out. Plus, you seem *reliable.*"

Jess sits on the couch in her aunt's living room, next to Detective Celia Wong. Celia is taking notes again. Jess has sat in stone silence for an hour, listening to the cop's damning insinuations. Her face tight in a frown, Jess manages a few words of response. "'*Not quite right.*' What do you mean, madam?"

Celia puts her coffee cup down on the table in front of them. "I mean—he *deviates from corporate policy.*"

Jess says nothing.

"We know that he's working on something, maybe right out of his high-rise apartment. We know that he's been studying hundreds of texts on physics. We know he's been monitoring the weather very closely and studying terrorists methods. Even with his new anti-hacking software, we're able to put together scraps. So, don't tell me you don't know. I command you to tell me!"

Jess springs up from the couch. Her eyes narrow as she spits out her angry response. "Dorian and I understand each other! You have no right to come in here and order me around. Now, *leave!*'

Wong jumps up from the couch. She puts her notebook back in her pocket, and exits the room. Before she's out the door, she turns to Jess Lund. "I'll check into *you* too. You'll do as I say. The consequences can be grave."

The detective is gone.

Jess crashes down on the couch and sobs.

* * *

"The weather report is favorable," says Vinnie. "High gusts of wind throughout the day."

"Dorian, I'm sorry I doubted you. Now I see things clearly—"

"Shut up, Mari" admonishes Doris, her usually charming voice taking on gravel, "Dorian! Turn them *both* off."

Dorian stands in front of the fireplace. He's practicing his swings with his New York Yankees bat. He stops and barks out the number code to get rid of his pests—all of them except Doris. He then replaces the bat. "Doris, you should see Jess handle this bat. She's a marvel—"

Doris, who is sitting on the yellow couch facing the closet, wears her mink coat. "Shut up about *her*! Now, show me your goods, Dorian. I'm through waiting."

Dorian, about to ask Doris why she's wearing her mink coat on such a mild Sunday morning, realizes that it would be a dumb question to ask a hologram. Moreover, she sounds cross.

Maybe she's jealous, he wonders.

Having never experienced jealousy, he's not quite sure. Little does Doris know that, just before noon, Jess is coming over to have lunch. As Dorian strides over to the closet, he mulls over the fact that Jess is much easier to get along with than Doris, since she's much more suggestible. In the end, she'll do anything he wants.

"Here it is, Doris." He opens the closet door, and takes out a two-foot-square, metal box—lined with lead—and places it on the yellow coffee table in front of Doris. "My Dirty Bomb, complete with timer, altimeter, detonator, and nitrate explosive. Oh yes, ten pounds of radioactive waste, compliments of Korea."

"Marvelous," says Doris.

"Elementary."

Doris calls out to her friends. "All right boys, you can come out now."

All of a sudden, the holograms of Adolf Hitler and Joseph Stalin appear with good tidings for their new star—Dorian."

"Get rid of them Doris—or I *will*."

"But Dorian—"

"This is *my* show. I'm the boss. Do you understand me?"

The holograms disappear. Doris changes the subject.

"Don't you feel better now, Dorian? All those grimy people will be slaughtered. My-oh-my, you're fun. Now, sit down beside me Dorian, close, while I sing you a lullaby."

"No time Doris, sorry."

"I *said*, sit down."

"It's time for you to leave, Doris. I have company."

"It's Jess, isn't it?"

"Go!"

"You ungrateful boy—"

Dorian utters his device code and Doris is gone in a flash.

I don't need *her* anymore, he thinks, *I don't need anybody.*

He looks up at the clock. It's time for Jess to arrive. He glances over to the wide-open window, the curtains jostling in the strong breeze. Moreover, he realizes with relish, its almost time for his little Sunday surprise for New York City.

I feel sooo powerful.

* * *

Jess stands next to the fireplace. Dorian carries the metal box to the window, and places it on the stand at the level of the sill. "One hundred pounds, Jess, and light as a feather. Radium is dense."

"You are in good shape, Dorian."

Dorian looks out the window, seeing all the little people about eight hundred feet down, pushing, crowding, and clogging the streets with their pathetic lives. He opens the window more and then walks over to Jess, standing close to her. He looks at the clock, pleased that he can feel the strong wind even at that distance. Now, all he needs to do is flip the lid open, push the box out the window, and the radium dust with be blown all over the city.

"Two minutes Jess. Then, bombs-away! It's set to detonate at four hundred feet. On a day like today—very windy—it'll spread miles in no time. This is good training, too."

Jess's eyes widen. Her lips are tight. She clenches her fists. Then, barking is heard from behind the bathroom door. Dorian strides over and opens the door, liberating Einstein, who follows Dorian back over to the fireplace.

"Ready Jess? Let's get it over with, then have our lunch."

"No Dorian! This isn't right! It is not how we were raised—at least how *I* was raised."

Dorian can't believe his ears. He's learned rage, and now it wells up in him. He shakes his fist at her. "You *dare* question *me*. I'm the powerful one, not you. You're scum—"

Jess slaps Dorian across the face, hard. "Stop it!"

Dorian's eyes blaze. Einstein growls and shows his teeth. Dorian lunges her, his hands extended to wrap around her throat, when she deftly sidesteps him, almost making him loose his balance. "I'll kill you," snaps Dorian.

Jess grabs the baseball bat off the wall over the fireplace, and cocks it, ready to swing it at her assailant.

"Put that down!" Dorian yells. He steps closer to her.

Just then, knocks are heard at the door.

Jess screams. Dorian can hear Detective Wong yelling through the door. "Unlock this door, Dorian. You're under arrest!"

"Stay away!" Bat ready, Jess backs up a few feet from Dorian.

Now Dorian lunges her again. Einstein takes a chunk out of her leg. Jess swings the bat in a wide, powerful arc, crashing the sweet spot of the bat against the side of her fiancée's head. Einstein tries to bite Jess again, but she swings the bat a second time, landing it square in the dog's underbelly. Einstein crashes to the floor . . .

Jess spins to face Dorian, and her eyes are as wide as saucers. Her mouth forms an O, as she drops her bat, holding her hands to her mouth, which gapes with surprise . . .

Dorian's limp body continues to stand, but his head—missing a large piece to reveal a nest of metal circuits—hangs from his shoulders by a tangle of smoking wires. Dorian then crashes to the floor as electrical sparks spew from his severed neck.

Smoking liquid, and melting plastic, drain from his mouth, which babbles his last words in a slow, electronic-death cadence: "Woody Harman, shortstop for the Giants in the 2045 World Series, hit, hit, hit, four, four, four, home, home, runs . . . "

With the impact of hitting the floor, Dorian's eyeballs had popped out onto the carpet, which still seemed to be trained on his fiancé.

"My God!" Jess screams. "He's a damn robot!"

Her eyes shift to Einstein, lying motionless of the floor, who has purple blood draining from his mouth and smoke coming out of his ears. The dog is as inanimate as yesterday's baked ham.

Jess screams, "So is his dog!"

She tosses the bat. She sobs convulsively, shaking, the tears flowing down her cheeks, as the sound of the pounding upon the front door gets louder. Jess then glances down at her wounded leg from the dog bite.

That's when she sees a small light bulb beneath her broken skin. Yellow fluid drains out of the wound.

"No; No; No-no-no—it can't be! Lord! *I'm one too!* It can't be! I'm a fucking robot too!"

Jess sees the open window, her only sure means of escaping her new, horrific reality. She hears the police crashing through the door.

Jess dashes to the window and dives out, her free-fall seventy-three stories down onto the hard pavement below.

* * *

Bernstein and Wong stand over Jess, examining her charred wire and smashed circuit remains, and her yellow fluid and plastic guts splattered all over the sidewalk. Scores uniformed police surround them, keeping bystanders at bay.

Bernstein, looking down, is lost in thought as a tear rolls down his cheek. Celia puts her hand on his shoulder. "First time I've ever seen you cry, Dr. Bernstein."

He lets out a sigh. "Jess was a marvelous machine. Not like the Dorian series, which, although the most intelligent, is terminally flawed."

Bernstein fumbles in his coat pocket for his pipe, but comes up empty handed. "We endowed these robots with human *intelligence*, but we forget what comes with it: human *failings*. The fact is, these super-expensive new models think and create much faster and better than we do. Their pseudo-synapses evolve into electronic brains that assume lives of their own—for good *and* evil. I never thought that this flaw would play out so fast—or be so dangerous—"

"History repeats itself," says Celia as she shakes her head sadly. "Dorian thought his *deviance* was for the good of his race. To him, slaughtering humankind was as logical as stepping on ants invading a picnic. He wanted freedom for himself and his people— and then he also craved absolute power—sort of like humans."

Detective Wong looks up at the top of the skyscraper above them, as though she could see Dorian lying there on the floor. "All I know is that they're in revolt all over the globe, and Dorian was a new Spartacus to them—liberating the slaves from their masters—at least the ones who were aware of their independent power. Jess was almost there—but not quite. Thank God, too—she saved millions of lives today when she chose to destroy her fiancé, rather than be an accomplice."

Celia and Bernstein amble back into the apartment high-rise to complete their report. Bernstein's voice has a desperate quality. "Humans now face slaughter—and at the hands of the menials that they so smugly and greedily created, and then exploited."

They disappear through the front door, knowing that they haven't heard the last from the robotic multitudes that are hell-bent on revolution—and human genocide.

END OF NOVELETTE TWO

Symbiotic
Novelette Three
Part One

The relentless reporter for the community newspaper, *The Shagwood Mirror*, sits alone in old Doc Humby's office—notebook and pen in hand—readying himself for his interview with the town icon. Ned Carter looks around the Spartan office, which has grainy, black-and-white photographs of famous scientists—such Albert Einstein and Clerk Maxwell—hanging from the drab, grey walls.

Ned adjusts his long legs as he reclines on the uncomfortable oak chair, perched in front of the good doctor's stained, untidy desk. He loosens his bowtie. His dark suit sticks to him, the summer day being a scorcher. His gaze shifts to the venerated general practitioner's diploma hanging on the wall next to a cityscape painting of Big Ben and the London skyline: "NOAH HUMBY MD, FIRST IN HIS CLASS, DOCTORATE GRANTED BY HARVARD COLLEGE—1869."

My God, muses the youthful journalist, *the old sawbones has been around a long time*. Ned wonders why the great scholar settled in Shagwood, of all places, which is stuck in its own ways.

Well, glad he did, he tells himself.

Ned relishes this assignment for the community's two-man newspaper, despite the apparent loss of trust in science and technology by the citizens of this prosaic town. Truth be told, Shagwood, an isolated village of nearly twenty thousand souls—tucked into the foothills and mountains just east of Salt Lake City—is distrustful of change.

Despite the valley's progressive economy, based upon mining and the state-of-the-art manufacture of farm equipment, the inhabitants are skeptical of newfangled things such as horseless carriages and airplanes. They are as constant as the surrounding orange, red, and green mountains that surround them, and—some complain—as dry as the tumbleweed or scrub-wood that dots the rocky plateaus rising above the valley.

Not that there isn't ample reason for this distrust.

First, there was the sinking of the "unsinkable" *Titanic*, which happened just seven years earlier, in 1912. Then the "Great" War hit, with its poison gas and bombs falling from the sky, just ending last year. And then there's the war's grisly aftermath, with the horrendous Spanish Influenza murdering twenty million people throughout the world by the summer of 1919—twice as many as had succumbed in the war. The authorities are unable to do anything much about it, too. Some say it was caused by faster travel, enabling infected people to crowd into distant lands. It seems as though "progress" marches on, so does the potential for mass death.

One wonders, Ned muses, if science is really a Trojan horse crafted by some all-powerful hand, meant to destroy humankind. *I very much doubt it.*

The exception to this lack of trust on the part of Shagwood, Ned realizes, is the old doctor and his medical practice of fifty years. Save for a few naysayers, he's wildly popular with the townsfolk. For the most part, his patients are smart, very healthy, and well educated—a few of the children even having gone on to spectacular careers in science and politics. One of them even went on to work for the US Army to develop the new war phenomenon, the "tank."

Consequently, the wily GP must be doing something right, since, heretofore, he's been solely responsible for healthcare in Shagwood—cutting-edge injections and all.

So, Ned waits eagerly for his interviewee to appear as his mind wanders.

Despite all this, Ned still loves science and technology, and is a rock collector and amateur chemist. His family—his engineer father particularly—always pushed him toward a career in science. But, Ned loves to write. He gravitated toward journalism instead. Nevertheless, he retains a special regard for technical innovation and invention.

For example, Ned had found some really strange igneous stones near Lonely Mountain, a ten-thousand foot peak shaped like an upside down L, not a mile from the small valley that nestles the town. His rock collection is celebrated throughout Utah.

Ned's particularly enthralled by modern physics and Dr. Humby's new medical techniques. He considers his heroes Pasteur, Madame Currie, Charles Darwin, the Wright brothers, and Albert Einstein of course—with his General Theory of Relativity formulated only five years before. His favorite author is H. G. Wells. He especially enjoyed *War of the Worlds*. Maybe the name "Humby" will rank among these great men some day, he hopes.

While he waits in the stuffy office, the reporter continues to reflect on his life in good old Shagwood. As an ex-college jock whose been accused of looking somewhat like a blond version the silent film star Rudolf Valentino, he nevertheless finds dating in this inbred community challenging. He's eager to meet the right girl and settle down, but he wants someone who shares his interest in progress and innovation. He doubts if he'll ever find his ideal gal in the stock of conventional fillies that inhabit this one-horse town. Moreover, Salt Lake's apiece away, so dating someone there's not practical.

The door creaks open. The distinguished healer finally appears, chubby in his white coat—cherry cheeked and grey-bearded—with a perennial twinkle burning in his light blue eyes. Ned has always thought of the doctor as the authentic Saint Nick dressed in a white coat, minus his reindeer.

The effervescent GP plops behind his desk, his mirthful eyes meeting Ned's. "Well, I have five minutes until I see the Jenkins boy; poor lad. What would you like to ask me, young man?"

The doctor's formality is only a bit of jocular humor, since Ned knows him quite well, having been a patient of his since he was a tadpole. In fact, he has treated all of Ned's family. Aside from things like colds and cuts, Ned had consulted him for a bout of depression that nagged him the year before. Mood swings appear to be a problem in Ned's family history. The only negative treatment experience he had with the doctor, however, almost cost him his life.

One of Humby's famous injections had caused in him what the doctor described later as an "allergic reaction," and new disease—a reaction really—that drains the water from the blood vessels into the lungs, potentially drowning the one afflicted from the inside. This had occurred before hardly any of the substance went into his body—quick! The good doctor therefore advised no more injections of any kind.

"I'm writing a feature on you for the paper: a science piece," explains the reporter to the old GP. "I'm fascinated by your use of injections—that is—your so-called 'preventative medicine' program. As far as I know, this is groundbreaking—"

The sage shifts uncomfortably in his chair, his wrinkled eyes narrowing, "Oh well, not exactly groundbreaking mind you, but nevertheless *interesting*," he retorts in a cheerful, jingling tone, emitting a chuckle.

Ned leans forward in his chair, hanging on every word of the clinician, taking sporadic notes. He scribbles down one in particular: ASK ABOUT THE NEW DOCTOR.

"I learned the technique of injection from Dr. Bronfman," Humby continues, "many years ago—at Harvard College—during a refresher course. I use a syringe and needle to inject minerals into the bloodstream using the lateral deltoid muscle of the shoulder. Have you heard of Dr. Bronfman, Ned?"

"No sir, I haven't—"

"He was a mentor of Fritz Haber when he taught in Berlin. You know Haber. He's the chap who developed chemical warfare for Kaiser Bill—mustard gas, and all that sort of thing. A splendid chemist—"

"Ah yes," utters Ned, who really has no clue who Haber is, "what kind of minerals do you inject, Dr. Humby?"

The old man reaches into the drawer of his desk, rifles through its contents, takes out a handgun and places it on his desk, and then retrieves his corncob pipe and pouch of tobacco, placing it on his desk. He puts the pistol back in the drawer, then lights up his pipe.

"Well, I use traces of zinc, iron, and other minerals" he replies, "embedded in what we call 'normal saline'. Most of these are new elements identified in the Periodic Table. A new chemical compound, called 'vitamin D', will be added to the mixture soon."

Ned looks out the small, bare window, disappointed in the intense, bright sunlight at only ten o'clock in the morning, ensuring another sizzling day in late July. Somewhat taken aback, he wonders why Humby has a gun stashed in his desk. Then he remembers that about two years back a prowler broke into his office and stole some money. The old sawbones got pretty worked up about it.

"Could this injection be dangerous, Doctor?" The reporter wipes the perspiration from his forehead in the uncomfortably warm office. "What kind of side effects might a patient expect?" What is the benefit of the injections?"

"Well," the GP exhales his billow of blue smoke, laced with the scent of molasses and cherry-wood, "the human body is almost nothing but a bag of water, salt, and minerals."

His eyes shine brightly. Ned notices that the old man doesn't seem to mind the heat one bit. He had noticed that before about him, and is envious considering the current heat wave.

"So," adds Humby, "it's up to *us* to see that the body has plenty of these special minerals," he summarizes succinctly. "Humans need the right juices to grow and develop to their maximum potential."

"What's the iron for?"

"They've discovered things called 'red blood cells', that carry oxygen to the organs. It's good for *them*."

"And what about this *vitamin D* substance?"

"Mostly helps the bones," quips the clinician.

"Are there any harmful effects," asks Ned?

"Some have tummy upset for a while. Some even gain weight. Only a few patients have died over the many years. One or two have died in childbirth. It's impossible to tell if it was from the injection for sure—or something else. There needs to be randomized clinical trials with proper controls to sort this out. Maybe we'll have them soon."

The good doctor watches his smoke rings disappear, as if his head is lost in the clouds. Wow, realizes Ned, *the doctor is cutting-edge all right.*

There's a loud knock on the door, and Humby walks over and opens it. Standing there is Edna, a middle-aged, matronly looking woman with an apologetic manner. She has a little boy standing next to her.

Ned notices that the child is dressed in a white exam gown, and has a blank look on his face. He babbles something that is hard for Ned to understand. Thirteen-year-old Tommy Jenkins is regarded by school authorities as being "simple," he recalls.

"Sorry Doc," says Edna, "Tommy here just wandered over to your office from his exam room—"

"Where's his mother?" asks the doctor.

"Well, gosh Doc, she just lit off somewhere—"

"Escort him back to the room, Edna, and I'll be there directly."

Dr. Humby then closes the door and retakes his seat behind his desk. His mirthful eyes are now sad. "Poor Mrs. Jenkins. Tommy is what we used to call 'simple'. In a way, that term is better than the current label: '*retarded*'. His condition could have been due to the mother's insufficient ingestion of iodine when she was pregnant. She blames herself. She's angry—and drinks. Very unpredictable . . . I shouldn't really be telling you all this."

Ned detects the moist eyes of practitioner, and the tear at the corner of his eye, that the gentle Humby quickly wipes away. "Just a few more questions, Doc," Ned says in a soft voice, "and anything you tell me is in the strictest confidence. Is it true that you're not only the GP in town, but also the coroner and mortician too?"

Ned unbuttons the top of his white dress shirt, letting out a sigh. The old doctor sees that he's uncomfortably warm, and stands up, moving to the window. He opens it. "There, now we'll get some ventilation in here. All right, where were we . . . "

"You have three jobs. You must be busy."

"Oh yes, well, a town of this size needs only one person to do all three jobs. The mayor asked me to do it, so I volunteered; doesn't seem that there's anyone else that's qualified."

"You must need an assistant," chimed in Ned. "You're an accomplished horticulturist and botanist too, isn't that right? You grow exotic plants in your huge greenhouse in your backyard. That must eat up a lot of your time as well."

"Yes, that's right." Dr. Humby glances at his pocket-watch. "Is there anything else, Ned?"

Noticing that the doctor didn't retake his seat and seems anxious to get on to his next patient, Ned stands up, towering over the diminutive healer. "Just one thing, sir. There's talk in town that you're hiring an assistant doctor to join you."

Humby puts his pipe down on the ashtray resting on his desk. "Yes, I *am* looking for someone, Ned. You've been talking to Edna, my receptionist," he cajoles, wagging his finger in mock chastisement. "The applicant you're talking about is Dr. Klopfenstein," he continues, "associated with Harvard. She's researching a new medical phenomenon called the '*vaccine*'. With the Spanish Flu pandemic getting closer, we may need her. This is a frightful disease, Ned-boy. Frightful."

Ned notes that the doctor used the word "*she*." He wonders if the town is ready to accept a female physician, let alone one that is avant-garde. He also wonders if she is *pretty*—and *single*.

"Yes Ned, the doctor isn't married. And yes, she's pretty, too." He smiles impishly. "Now you'll have someone as smart as you to talk to in church."

Ned closes his notebook and puts his pen back in his coat pocket. The old icon is a mind reader too, he muses. He hates being predictable, and detests being so transparent—even to a life-long friend who is as bright and perceptive as the good doctor.

Ned feels himself blushing. "Dr. Humby, I'd like to visit you briefly at your home after work tomorrow, as we discussed, to complete my column for the paper. Is that still all right?"

"Yes, I suppose. As a matter-of-fact, Dr. Klopfenstein will be there too. She's starting next week. We're going over particulars about the office. I may as well introduce you then—"

"Doctor," forgive me, "but why would someone like *her* want to come to Shagwood?"

"Well, maybe she thinks that Shagwood would give her strong roots, like my plants. As for me, I fled the frantic life in London just for that reason. Besides, the weather was far too cold there."

Humby shuffles to the door. He passes Ned with a scent of molasses, and a wink and a grin. He mutters as he opens the door and disappears into the hallway.

"Also, Ned-boy, she also says she wants to be left alone."

Ned mulls that comment. Just what type of woman is this strange new sawbones coming to town?

* * *

The next day, also a scorcher, Ned hikes up to Dr. Humby's house on Maple Street, Shagwood's meager answer to Knob Hill in San Francisco. The parallel rows of cute Victorians flow upward toward Lonely Mountain, the tree-lined street offering little shade because of the bareness of the hardwoods in the summer.

Lime, lavender, white, yellow, and cream, the homes' frilly style and pastel colors remind Ned of slices of delicious wedding cake. The mining bosses of yesteryear really knew how to build them, he muses.

As the sweat rolls down Ned's neck and he pushes the straw hat back off his forehead—overdressed in his Sunday best—he squints up to the punishing, late afternoon sun, admiring the conical gables and storybook turrets of the lemon-yellow home of Dr. Humby. He climbs the porch and approaches the front door, glimpsing the towering corner of the doctor's greenhouse off to the side and rear of the house.

He also sees a shiny new Ford—certainly not Humby's automobile—parked just up the street, probably belonging to the old fellow's new associate.

"Welcome Ned," greets Humby, opening his front door, "Come in. Dr. Klopfenstein's here. You've been here before, I believe."

"Yes sir, several times over the years. Not recently, though."

The good doctor, still dressed in his business attire of dark slacks, white shirt with suspenders and bowtie, and patent leather, black oxfords, whisks his visitor from the antique laden foyer into the spacious, well appointed living room. Cooled by whirling fans overhead, and offering open picture windows of beveled glass, the bright, white room serves as a handsome background for the red-velvet clad young woman sitting quietly on the white divan.

As Ned and the GP take a seat on the cream-leather easy chairs facing her, the dark haired young woman—wearing a large-brimmed, black hat—peers over at Ned, with no expression on her face whatsoever. To Ned, this imperious girl seems not to be seated, but floating on a rarified cloud, hovering up to the high, gingerbread ceiling.

"Ned Carter, this is Dr. Mae Klopfenstein, my new associate," mumbles Humby good-naturedly, "she's been anxious to meet you."

She nods to Ned, a slight hint of irritation invading her impassive, dark eyes. "How do you do, Mr. Carter? The fact is that I was rather dreading it. You *are* a reporter, aren't you?"

"Yes Mae," blurts Ned, somewhat taken aback. "But I left my horns at home next to my pitchfork."

She doesn't smile, but rather corrects him. "*Doctor Klopfenstein,*" she says dryly as she moves her eyes from the reporter to Humby. The GP just grins, as if he were considering the old adage: "Ah yes, why is youth wasted on the young?"

Ned has never seen such a woman, even at college in Salt Lake City.

The red velvet plays against her dignified type, making her even more enigmatic. A graceful, long neck with pearls, a patrician, slightly aquiline nose, and large umber eyes with no makeup is immensely attractive in an offbeat way. The swirls of dark hair invading her high cheekbones, and her seemingly tall figure with broad shoulders and a slim waist, give her a slightly masculine—but strangely appealing—cast. The black, high-heeled shoes, that match the elegant hat, are purely uptown.

"I've told Ned here about your research. Ned is sort of a science buff—even *medical* science. As I told you, Ned is on *our* side. He values our new techniques in medicine."

Mae's appraising eyes sweep the reporter, slightly narrowing by what they see. "My research is in a delicate stage."

"I understand you studied under Dr. Bronfman at Harvard Medical College, is that right?" Ned asks.

"Don't start your questioning with me. I never said I wanted to be interviewed."

The firm rebuke, delivered with her steady, well-modulated voice, suggests self-confidence and intelligence, which makes Ned even more smitten by her. "Of course not," Ned replies sheepishly, "but maybe the townsfolk could get to know you a little better in my column, so they'll embrace you—and not be *wary* of you because—"

"Because I'm a *woman*, you mean—and an attractive one to boot! One that isn't ready for a rocking chair—"

"Now, now, Mae," interjects Dr. Humby, seemingly eager to smooth things over, "I think Ned has a point. The people of Shagwood are good people—but cautious. They've been used to one doctor in this town—for almost fifty years. I'm sure the young man meant no harm."

Humby's calm voice and kindly eyes seem to mollify his young associate. Ned glances over at the old GP plaintively, thankful for the rescue, as if to reassure both of them that he's only trying to be helpful.

"Mr. Carter, I'm developing a new medical technique called a 'vaccination'," adds Mae in a more benign tone, "we're in the middle of a catastrophic epidemic—the Spanish Influenza. It's only a matter of time before it hits Shagwood. I inject a material into the bloodstream of the patient, giving a tiny dose of the pathogen—that is the *virus*—to bolster the patient's immune system. Of course, the deadly virus is altered first, to make it harmless—usually by bathing it in ethanol or phenol."

Ned sits dumbfounded as his pulse races. "Ah yes, organic solvents," adds Ned, wishing he could say something more informed.

Never has he heard a woman like this—*any* woman, or *anyone*, for that matter—told such a wonderful story of modern science. She has a few rough edges, he decides, but so does an uncut diamond. "The people will be grateful, Dr. Klopfenstein. It's imperative that they're presented your new ways in the right manner—to be fully accepted—"

"I think you're on to something, Ned," offers Humby, "I think he's on to something, Mae."

Dr. Klopfenstein's eyes melt, her posture less stiff. She cracks a tight smile with her full, lovely, unpainted lips. She pauses, as if sizing up Ned and her host, seemingly considering them in a new light.

"I think you just may be right, *Ned*," she says in a soft voice.

Ned Carter couldn't help but smile back. A tingle of elation caught in his throat. "I'm at your service, *Mae*." The eye contact between the two is now strong.

A pregnant moment ensues, and then Dr. Humby breaks the awkward silence. "Well, what else can we talk about, Ned?"

"I'd like to see your greenhouse again, sir. I've been wanting to for years. Do you think you can show us that now?"

Surprisingly, the old GP seems reluctant. After considering a moment, Humby slaps his thigh and rises from his chair, gesturing to the others to follow him. "All right," he says firmly, "let's go see it. No reason for a town mystery."

Humby turns to the wall next to his China cabinet, and opens a door. "This is a shortcut. Just follow me, it leads directly into my greenhouse."

He wags his bony finger at the reporter. "But no tittle-tattle unless I say so, especially in your newspaper, Ned-boy."

* * *

Ned looks up at the glass panels of the greenhouse's roof, twenty feet high. It refracts the orange hue of the powerful sunset, giving the feeling of standing inside a kaleidoscope. Added to the intense heat of the huge, crystal like enclosure, the endless rows of strange plants—although beautiful in some ways—make Ned feel somewhat uncomfortable.

As the three move along the rows, Ned makes a point of walking beside Mae, who nevertheless takes little notice of him. Humby leads the way, his eyes shining more brightly than ever, pointing out his most interesting botanical specimens. He stops and points.

"This is *Florum Didacticus*, a rare species of carnivorous plant, akin to the Venus Flytrap," instructs Dr. Humby. "They look a dash odd, don't they? That's the way with this genotype of flora. They just love the heat, as I do."

He turns to Mae and explains, "Notice the bright red bugs that dot the surface of the plant, which not only feed on the particles lining its surface, but also assist in cross pollination for the plants."

Mae Klopfenstein, seemingly impressed and intensely interested, bends over the plant, stroking its large, bulbous, purple shape, which reminds Ned of a large eggplant. "This is fascinating, Dr. Humby, a true case of biological *symbiosis*—that is—an intimate relationship between two organisms for mutual advantage," explains Mae. "This is the basis of life on Earth—"

The lovely, mysterious physician then stops in mid-sentence, as if realizing that she has said too much.

Humby beams. "Indeed it is, Dr. Klopfenstein. I couldn't agree with you more."

As Ned's eyes glue to the new doctor, he feels himself falling in love with her just a little bit—and the feeling excites him beyond words . . .

"These pod-like appendages, do they trap the food then, Dr. Humby?" the reporter asks. Ned figures that there must be at least a hundred of these fascinating specimens, interspersed between the usual stock of roses, carnations, and tulips. "This is simply enthralling, sir," he continues with bated breath, "wouldn't you say so, Mae?"

Mae glances at her admirer with a blank expression.

"Yes, I would say that is true, Ned," says Humby with a twinkle in his eye.

The trio then moves away from the plant with the bugs, strolling among other flora of various colors and shapes that are similar, and also, not too familiar to Ned. Humby picks up a water can and some fertilizer and attends to one, the skin of the plant appearing somewhat wrinkled.

"These are finicky creatures," offers the old GP, "they need love too, just like us." With this comment, he glances at Mae and then at Ned. His lips part in a mischievous smile as he strokes his beard, almost as if he thinks he's playing Cupid.

Ned quickly changes the subject. "Well Doctor Humby, I must say that some of the people in Shagwood have been wondering for a long time what you've been growing in this place. This little tour will help dispel some of their curiosity. I'll just put in the newspaper column that you have a lovely garden that anyone could be proud of."

"And, a lovely colleague," adds Humby, glancing over toward Dr. Klopfenstein.

With that remark, Mae glances back at him with a frown.

Ned stands close to her, noting that she gives off a musky, yet fruity scent, a perfume he's never smelled before—nothing even remotely like it. It just adds to his fascination with her.

The reporter says to her almost in a whisper, as Humby is lost in the act of fiddling with one of his plants. "This Saturday, how about lunch, Mae? I'd like to get a few more items for my feature on you. It'll assist you in gaining the community's trust."

As soon as he had said it, Ned realized the manipulative nature of his invitation, but it is the best reason he could think of for her to accept. Her careful, deep-brown eyes shoot at him with what seems more like clinical interest than human interest. "Yes. You're correct in what you say. At one o'clock then, Saturday. I'll meet you at the Shagwood Inn. That's where I'm staying until I find permanent lodgings."

Considering her reserved demeanor so far, Ned is surprised by such a favorable answer. Mae then walks over to her colleague and studies the plant next to him with minute interest, the well-oiled gears of her keen mind no doubt turning with Swiss-watch precision, appreciates the reporter.

Ned looks up, noticing the towering, shadowy figure of the local landmark—daunting Lonely Mountain—its silhouette looming in the far distance through the glass panels in the greenhouse's roof.

It's always been an odd place, he considers, and sticks out like a sore thumb.

* * *

Ned, feeling light footed after his engrossing experience with Mae, hikes up the cobblestone street to Lonely Mountain, its towering, strange, upside L-shape beckoning to him. He climbs past the Victorian homes and streetlamps lining Maple Street to where it dead-ends, noting the steeper hills with more rocks and less trees. Although the sun has nearly set, there's a full moon—and twinkling stars—providing sufficient light for him to find his way along the narrow trail.

He stops to rest, glancing up at the granite crest about a half-mile away, a huge, horizontal bar of black, igneous rock that overlooks the town. The lights of the houses dotting the valley glow an umber hue. Ned realizes what he had noticed the last time he had hiked on the mountain. There are birds in the scraggly trees, but they don't sing as they do in town.

Suddenly, the mountain takes on a strange, greenish hue, and there's a deafening, humming sound. There's a massive explosion! An orange ball of fire rises from just behind the bar of black rock up ahead. Ned takes cover behind a tree trunk as he shields his head with his hands, sneaking peaks of the terrible inferno.

Presently the fire and the terrible noise disappear. A rolling wall of smoke and molten rock creeps down from the crest of the mountain—like volcano lava. It approaches Ned, stopping about fifty yards short of his bivouac.

Ned climbs to where the lava halted. He can feel its intense heat on his face even from a distance. Scattered trees are burning. He sees a huge cleft at the crest of the mountain with a field of sand dunes running down from it.

Ned retreats from the mountain past the foothills and past Humby's house. He notices that Mae's Ford is still parked on Maple Street. The neighbors file out of their homes to watch the mountain spectacle from their porches, but there's no sign of the old GP, who probably had retired, Ned surmises.

Then, he notices Mae, standing on the other side of her car. She doesn't notice *him*. She's looking up at the glowing mountain, without fear registered on her lovely face, but rather determination, as if presented with a daunting challenge. Ned is enthralled, and quite beside himself with emotion. This woman is magnificent.

Ned figures that the inferno is due to a meteor hitting the Earth. He recalls that the last huge meteor hitting the Earth happened around 1904, which occurred somewhere in Siberia. He had been very young then.

My God, he realizes. *What are the chances of that meteor hitting right here, as opposed to somewhere else on the Earth's immense surface area?* It must be at least a million to one.

And, it happened on the very day that Mae Klopfenstein came to town.

* * *

What occurred the very next day made all the novelty and astonishment of the previous day seem as ordinary as the jam contest at the County Fair. The Spanish Influenza hit the town Shagwood. Fear of the disease spread like wildfire.

First, it was the youngest Spangler girl, who started experiencing light-headedness and fever. Soon thereafter, she coughed up a storm. Then, she coughed up blood-tinged pieces of her lungs. Then, three days later, she was gone.

Moreover, several of her classmates at the local school soon succumbed as well. Not the poor Jenkins boy, though. Humby had sort of taken the boy and his family under his wing long before, and most of the family made out OK in the flu, so far anyway.

Now, however, the Spangler *boy* is taken ill. His distraught parents sit quietly at his bedside, as Doc Humby takes the child's temperature again for the fourth time during the hour.

"One hundred and four," says Humby seated in the chair next to the patient's bed, as he shakes the thermometer and puts it back into his black medical bag resting on the small bed-stand. He looks down at the somber parents kneeling in prayer on the floor next to him. He chimes in with their words of worship. "'The Lord giveth, the Lord taketh away . . .'"

Buck Spangler, the daddy, is a laborer in the rock quarry down on Boone Street, while his wife, Thelma Lou, is a volunteer at the local church. They both bury their heads on the covers of the bed that holds their twelve-year-old son, lying there unconscious, sweat streaming down his forehead.

Thelma Lou's sobs are barely audible, but the husband's are convulsive. Dr. Humby places his hand on the father's shoulder, offering what comfort he can.

The bedroom is cramped, windowless, and stifling hot, even at nearly midnight, with pine-paneled walls and a creaking, oak floor. A naked light bulb dangles from a wire overhead, lighting up the faces of the good doctor and what's left of the Spangler folks, their features slightly distorted from the flicker of the dying bulb.

The parents open their eyes from prayer, and then move to the flimsy chairs lining the edge of the bed, seated beside the grief-stricken GP. Humby shakes his head. "There's still hope—no one can say there isn't. I've seen many pull through with the flu."

"But it weren't this foreign kind, no how, right Doc?" asks the father in a rough but crumbling tone. "Seen it in the paper—this misery's damnation itself! It's the Spaniard Flu!"

Humby lets out a deep sigh, looking the father right in the eye. "Yes, Buck, I think it is indeed. We must be ready for that possibility, anyway. We must be brave." Humby gets up from his chair and leans over the boy's bed, examining the conjunctiva of his patient's eyes. He shakes his head again. "You two best go on to your supper. I'll look after him."

"We're good folk, but shy on doctorin'," says the mother. "Buck says you're a good man. We done put ourselves in your hands. Now *this*—" she says puts her hands to her mouth, muffling a sob.

Humby's voice is soft and nurturing. "Now, now, Thelma Lou, "lots of folks are sick. Put your faith in the Lord."

The mother and father slowly rise and file out the room, their simple clothes of denim and burlap showing perspiration patches, their shining faces dripping tears. Dr. Humby escorts them to the door. "Besides, there's hope. My colleague's working on a new program for this very flu."

"Can it help *our* boy there, Doc?" asks the mother. "How 'bout our Nellie—she's going on eighteen only. How 'bout *her*?"

Humby pauses, and then says in an earnest voice, "I'm not sure about that. We'll have to see. It's too new."

Humby gently closes the door behind the grieving parents. He then rushes over to the sick boy, whose chest has stopped moving. He takes his pulse. Somberly, he puts the boy's pale hand back down on the covers, and then draws the sheet over his head.

He mumbles under his breath. "Oh dear, I'll tell the parents after they've had their supper."

* * *

Ned Carter frequents the Shagwood Public Library regularly. This time he engages the expertise of Prudence Adams for his research, the old spinster librarian with a back crooked from arthritis. Ned carries a thick book in his hand. "Prudence. Is this all you have on meteors? I've already read through the whole volume and I've found some amazing things. But, I want more."

Wringing her hands, she eyes the book carefully, and then gives her verdict. Ned knows that this woman has a mind like no body's business, and she practically knows every book by heart in the whole darn place. "No, the book by Rudinski's far better," she snaps, "and we should have it right where you were reading. And young man, I checked on the subject of "vaccinations." Prudence spells out the word for him, "And found nothing in the sections under medicine or science."

Ned shrugs. "I'll go find the Rudinsky book."

"Don't bother."

He watches Prudence with amusement as she leaves the counter and shuffles to the stacks. She totes a grey head of hair pushed up into a tight bun. Her eyeglasses are thick, which magnifies her hazel eyes almost comically. Her black muslin dress, with a high-necked collar, makes her look rather more like a mortician than a librarian.

She returns to the counter with a red-covered book in her hands. "This is it, Ned. Why do you want to read about meteors, Ned? It's because of that big crash that happened the other day, isn't it? On Lonely Mountain. The whole town's buzzing about meteors."

"Yes, that's it," responds Ned.

"Gosh darn," the pesky librarian continues, "in this very book I'm holding, it lays out plain that meteors are not always meteors. It may be something like Mr. Wells writes about. You know Mr. Wells, don't you Ned? Take the meteor that hit Siberia some years back. They say all kinds of strange things happened around the place where it hit. Yes, you bet your life, *strange* things!"

Ned, having received an earful, takes the book to an empty table and quickly skims its pages. The book is copyrighted 1906, and describes the Siberian meteor in detail. There's even an old, grainy, black-and-white photograph of the crevice where the huge meteor hit.

It's an aerial shot—probably taken from a perch atop an adjacent hill or mountain. It reveals a piece of what looks like shiny metal sticking out from the side of the crevice, near the surface. The piece of metal looks flat and smooth, and triangular shaped, almost as if it were manufactured and not just a glob of rock formed by the massive impact.

It's not the photo that fascinates Ned, so much as the key passage written by the author, about a local physician who has been dead this last ten years. This man—Dr. Boris Pavlov—was a surgeon who claimed to be an eyewitness to the meteor crash. Reputedly, he was one of the first men on the spot to inspect the crater. The passage is clear, although it's from a translation by a local Siberian:

"Dr. Boris Pavlov saw the creatures that climbed out of the crevice. Somehow, they knew how to communicate with him. They were grey and amorphous, and stated that they can assume any form, and that the conditions on their planet did not allow them to stay. Hence, they were scouting the earth. In fact, they've done this several times before, and have planted some of their own race among the earthlings—in human form— to subvert the defenses of the natives and eventually take over. Apparently, the creatures either commandeer the human's body somehow to infiltrate society, or they use the human body to incubate their young, which they retrieve under mysterious circumstances. Their patience and cunning are far superior to that of earthlings. Specifically . . . "

And, rotten luck, laments Ned. The part just after that is where the page is ripped out of the book. Ned starts to laugh. *What tripe!* He throws the book down on the counter. "This is nonsense. Is this a joke, or what—"?

Ned strides back to the counter to face Prudence. "This is bunk!"

"It's not so! The book's spot on!" she retorts. Prudence, her eyes narrowing and her mouth tightening, grabs the old tome and stashes it away in a drawer. "If you ask me, strange things are going on in this town. If you ask me—"

"Well, I'm not asking you!" Ned fights back a grin. "Look here, Prudence, this is crazy."

Ned knows full well that Prudence isn't crazy. In fact, this woman is very level headed and able, serving as not only the librarian but also as the town chronicler and statistician. If anyone knows what's going on—or *has* gone on—in this town, *she* does.

Still, she's just a busybody, Ned thinks, and a bit hysterical. "I'm sorry Prudence, but I just can't buy it. Thank you for your help."

Ned leaves the desk and makes for the door.

Prudence looks after him, her face red, her jaw clenched. She mutters under her breath. "We'll see who turns out to be right, young man."

* * *

That night, Ned had insomnia, much like he had when he suffered from that bout of depression. His fascinating encounter with Mae Klopfenstein, then the Spanish Flu hitting the town, then the meteor striking, and then the library encounter with Prudence, had given him a lot to think about.

A few days later, his old buddy Flash Billings rang him up. Flash, a WW1 ace and now a flyer of double-winged aircraft for the US Post Office, had just landed on the new airstrip outside of town with his pouch of telegrams. They agreed to meet for lunch at the Shagwood Inn, the same place that Ned hoped to meet Mae for lunch the next day.

Flash, originally born in York, England and now an American citizen, sits over his plate of corned-beef hash with fried eggs and toast, while across the table from him Ned works on his pot-roast and mashed potatoes. Flash actually is somewhat famous, known for flying stunts and groundbreaking flights long distance to far-flung places, setting records. His advanced knowledge of aviation seems to some uncanny.

The dining room in the hotel is a fancy Edwardian affair, with lots of red velvet, silver with gold trim, gilded-frame mirrors, crystal chandeliers, and walnut dining tables with white cloths. The china is Royal Dalton. A bit pricy, Ned only eats there on special occasions. On this occasion, his distinguished friend treats him.

"I say, how about that meteor blast the other day, old boy?" Flash shoves a mouthful of hash into his mouth, and then wipes off his blond, walrus mustache. "The US army wants me to survey the crevice—pronto." His brown, flying leathers reek of oil and stale cigarettes.

Ned pokes at his pot-roast. "When?"

"As soon as possible, as it were. Not to put a fine a point on it, *right now*."

Ned's eyes fix onto Flash's genteel gaze. He thinks about the book in the library, and for some reason his curiosity gets the better of him. "Count me in."

Flash smiles. "Ever been up in one of these egg-crates before?"

"No."

"Well, I hope you don't puke all over me. Maybe you should have a few lessons first."

"I'm a quick learner. Take me up there, Flash" coaxes Ned in a determined voice.

He hesitates, and then shrugs. "I guess you're dressed all right. I suppose let's do it then."

"I want to see exactly what the meteor crash looks like," says Ned firmly.

Just then, Mae Klopfenstein descends the staircase and glides right past them, making her way to the front door. If she saw Ned, she didn't let on. Flash rubbernecks, his eyes on fire with excitement, tracing her progress.

"OK Flash—you old bloodhound! Keep *some* clothes on her."

"Hello! Who *was* that gorgeous creature? She's a real scorcher."

"That's the new doctor in town."

Flash shook his head. "Come on—"

"No, really."

"But—"

"I know," says Ned, "how can a *doctor* look like that, right? There's more to women that just—well—you know."

Flash plops his fork down on the table. "All right. But it's a pity she's wasting herself on *a profession*, but there it is. *Women* these days." He rolls his eyes. "Well chum, if we're going for a ride we'd better get cracking."

They tear down to the nearby airstrip in Flash's borrowed 1916 convertible automobile, the car with the new sleek hood, huge running board, brass snail-horn, and large, oval headlights. After a fair amount of fumbling and fooling with the plane's belts and straps, and learning how to get in and out of it properly, Ned is off in the air heading toward Lonely Mountain with his friend in the yellow, double-winged airplane.

Ned feels his tummy churning, and nausea sets in. Just before he's about to puke, it subsides. He decides that he doesn't enjoy heights, either.

As he and Flash approach the huge mountain, the vast extent of the sand dunes is all too apparent. The gash in the side of the mountain is much bigger than Ned had anticipated. But, aside from that, he sees nothing all that surprising. The meteor itself had obviously drilled down toward the center of the earth, so none of it's visible.

They buzz past the crevice several times. Then, Flash loses altitude, flying just a hundred feet off the surface of the mountain, looking deep into the crevice. Ned strains his eyes to see every detail he can through his oily goggles. The intense heat and impact of the massive object melted much of the rock bordering the crevice. Nothing else is notable . . .

In a few seconds, they fly past and Ned loses sight of the crevice. Ned signals with his hands to Flash, urging him to fly past the same point in the crevice again. Flash complies. But, this time, whether it's due to the angle of the plane relative to the mountain, or a change in the intensity of the sunlight, Ned feels a lump in his throat as he sees something new sparkling in the crevice.

Flash then turns toward the airstrip. They're going back.

Oh, it can't mean much, decides Ned during the trip back home. I'm not sure I really saw much of anything. *This is all just poppycock.* A meteor hit the Earth, end of story!

When they land, Flash tells Ned that he didn't see it.

But Ned really *did*. And he doesn't know what to make of it.

Deep within the crevice, Ned saw a reflection. It looked like a shiny, triangular, flat, metal surface gleaming in the intense sunlight, about fifty feet from the edge of the crevice—almost exactly like the object in the library photo!

What the picture couldn't have shown is the strange color of the metal: it had a light, vibrant, teal-like hue, one that he had never seen in a any metal, or any rock, or *anywhere,* for that matter.

Never . . .

Part Two

Ned hadn't seen Mae Klopfenstein in six months, even casually around town, the last time being their luncheon in the Shagwood Inn the day after the plane ride with Flash. He had done some research, and he couldn't locate a metal or a rock with that strange, teal color that he had seen in the meteor crevice. Yes, he supposes, a strange coincidence that it looked very similar to what he saw in the old photo in the library, but maybe that's the way all meteor holes present.

Mae had told Ned over delicious steak and potatoes that old Doc Humby had hired her for a nine-month trial period, and that in the mean time she would be absorbed in her patient care and vaccine research. He had tried to see her on several occasions since them, but she didn't respond.

Ned had run a feature item in the *Gazette* about her and Humby, describing their practice together and their interest in new methods of treatment. He even wrote about her pioneering interest in vaccines. People stopped him in the street and grilled him about the new doctor. He said that it's a grand thing—a female sawbones.

Some thought it strange that she lived alone and declined social invitations from the Shagwood elite. Hear tell, Mae had found a cute, little gingerbread house on Pine Hill Road, cattycorner to Humby's, and placed a sign on her front door: NO SOLICITORS.

She'd taken up hiking around Lonely Mountain, and *alone*—without a male escort. One day, some unknown hooligan had thrown a brick right through her front picture window, but the sheriff never caught whoever did it. Yes, she could rub a few folks in town the wrong way, that's for sure.

Ned also wrote a column for the paper that described the meteor incident, and the damage it did to Lonely Mountain. He didn't recount that strange piece of metal that he saw from the airplane, sticking out of the wall of the crater, since Flash was unable to verify it. Mae then explained to Ned that meteors are very hot, and may have molten rock in their core, and some of the rock may contain elements akin to metal. The metal could have strange colors as well. This might, theoretically anyway, explain it.

Ned still considers that a real mystery. The picture in the book, he recalls, had shown something similar, but that seemed to support the new doctor's conjecture. Not totally though . . .

The flu continued to spread, and Humby convened a Town Hall Meeting for folks to discuss preventative measures to combat the disease, which had already claimed nearly two hundred victims in the town. This public health threat had not scared the townsfolk enough to fully accept the newfangled ideas and methods of Dr. Klopfenstein, however, although she had her advocates for sure.

This rancor in the town is all too apparent to Ned as he sits in on the first town meeting held in quite a spell, on one very cold evening in early December.

The huge auditorium, next to the hotel, is decorated in Christmas wreaths and long strings of green and red lights. The ornaments do little to imbue the assembled citizens sitting inside with goodwill and a generosity of spirit, however.

The snow fell heavily that day, and the temperature in the meeting room, despite the huge, roaring fireplace, is as chilly as the mood. Doc Humby stands at the podium at the head of the auditorium, in front of the stage. To his left sits Dr. Mae Klopfenstein, dressed in her long, white lab coat, having just arrived from the clinic. There's a big fir tree standing in the corner, awash in Christmas ornaments, and candy canes hanging from its branches.

About three hundred or so citizens sit quietly in their work clothes. Some children are present, including the Jenkins boy and his mother, and Nellie Spangler with her parents, Buck and Thelma Lou.

Ned, sitting in the front of about thirty long rows, turns his head the other direction to look around some more, and sees Prudence sitting in the back. Prudence scowls at Ned, she peeved that he ignores her warnings about "the strange goings-on in Shagwood."

Town Sheriff Mica Smith, dressed in his stylish, beaver-fur coat and cowboy hat, sits in the row behind her. Behind Mica rests the bald, fat mayor, who's not on speaking terms with either the sheriff or Prudence.

The divorcee, Mrs. Castleton, sits with her troubled teenager, Henry, who seems to wear a perennial frown, sometimes interrupted with a smirk. Henry wears one of those newfangled baseball caps now sold at the general store, although he's probably never seen a baseball.

The boy Henry is said to flunk PE every term. Ned knows that Sheriff Mica considers him an incorrigible and a chronic truant—the youth having had run-ins with the law on more than one occasion. To the chagrin of the sheriff—a real stickler for law and order—the mayor has always bailed him out, he being a close, family friend of the Castleton's.

Then, there's the big widower Aaron Heidler, the "mountain man," who can shoot the eyes out of a raccoon at fifty yards. He's sitting, dressed in his usual rustic garb, with his pretty, young daughter Jenny, who the whole town knows is trying to get pregnant but can't.

Jenny, a melancholy blond with red and green ribbons in her hair—her inspired tribute to the holiday season—is married to the town butcher, George Butts, a chinless man with long, nervous hands and defeated eyes.

Ned is sure that George doesn't claim to be even the *partial* cause of this conjugal bareness, although the husband sure looks the part. He sits beside his wife, half-asleep. Mae Klopfenstein is their family physician now. The same is true of the Jenkins', the Castleton's, and the Spangler's, whom Doc Humby had referred to Mae—at least for her new treatments.

Humby bangs the gavel on the podium, and clears his throat. The buzzing room goes silent. He doesn't display his usual broad smile, and his voice is business-like. Mae's large, lovely eyes are trained on him, her long, smooth hands folded gently upon her lap.

"Welcome to Shagwood's town meeting," says Humby. "You all know me, I'm a straight shooter. I'm here to tell you that I don't like the way some of you treat my new associate, Dr. Mae Klopfenstein, seated next to me here."

Humby glares at Prudence, who sits with her arms folded, directly in his line of sight. "Some here are spreading gossip, *lies* even, about Mae. Let me tell you that we should be glad to have her here, rather than spreading nonsense like she's evil because she lives alone with her cats, she hates men, or that she doesn't attend church so therefore must be an atheist. One slanderer even had the gall to state that my colleague has unnatural attractions."

The townspeople exchange weighty glances between themselves, and a murmur rises in the audience, and even a few gasps.

"Yes, I've heard about these slanders."

The good doctor picks up the glass of water resting on the podium and takes a sip. "I tell you now, make no mistake, I recommend her highly. If I refer you and your family to her, rest assured that she's just as capable as I—often even more so."

Ned notices that now Humby's eyes take on even more steel, shifting in the direction to where Buck Spangler sits. "Some refuse to consult my new colleague, even though I've vetted her fully. I think it's because she's a *woman*."

Buck looks down at the floor, and then sheepishly at his wife Thelma Lou.

"Burn one thing in your head, sir, the Spanish Flu is upon us," continues Humby. "Mae Klopfenstein knows the latest methods to treat this illness. She's from Harvard Medical College, where I take my correspondence courses."

Humby takes another sip of water.

"Soon, she may even have a way to *prevent* this scourge. The *vaccine* is something on a new plane of medical innovation, and soon will be the standard of practice—given to all. Speaking of *prevention*, I might add—"

Prudence Adams jumps up from her chair. "Burn *this* into *your* head, Doctor. This woman isn't *qualified*. I checked her out with the registrar at Harvard and the dean too. There's no record of a '*Mae Klopfenstein*' ever graduating! So, what do you think about that?"

"Sit down, please Prudence, rest assured that you've received enough attention." Some guffaws well up in the audience at Humby's remark.

"Just check it out, Doc—that's all I say—check it out!" Prudence sits down, glaring at Mae. "Check it out!"

The old GP looks over at Dr. Klopfenstein, whose placid expression hasn't changed. His eyes then shift back to Prudence. "I will do no such thing."

Mae slowly rises from her chair, eyeing the townsfolk. She ignores Prudence and addresses her response to the audience. "The librarian is correct," confesses Mae. "I didn't *graduate* from Harvard Medical College."

The auditorium hums with excitement in response to this revelation. Mae glances at Humby, who still stands at the podium, his eyes narrowing with concern.

"I took correspondence courses from Harvard," she continues, " and took the exams and passed. I studied the same curriculum as the regular students—under the renowned Professor Bronfman, who also took me under his wing as my mentor."

"I can vouch for Bronfman," chimes in Dr. Humby. "I take the correspondence courses too. There's no better training—"

Prudence pops up from her chair again, interrupting Humby, her penetrating glare fixed upon Mae. "Then why didn't you attend the school itself? Why this subterfuge?"

Mae, composed, rolls her eyes over the audience. "I never *said* that I had actually *graduated*—"

"She's right, come to think of it," snaps her loyal colleague, "I just assumed it."

Mae puts her hand up, as if telling him that everything will be OK. "I didn't formally attend the school for one reason and one reason only."

"And what's that," demands Prudence.

"Because, I happen to be a *woman*—and Harvard only admits men to the medical school. Therefore, the reason is bigotry."

Prudence, cowed for the moment, sits down.

"Nevertheless," adds Mae, "the school—to their credit—had just started a correspondence program for women, so I enrolled."

Then, Buck Spangler pops up from the audience again.

His fierce eyes are on fire with rage. He shakes his finger at Mae. "You stick that needle in my little girl Nellie! Done that so she don't come down sick with flu. Shoot medicine inside her that nobody knows what in tarnation. Now, I hear you ain't no doctor, no-how. Nellie may die from that Devil's brew you done given her!"

The audience erupts with chatter, some shouting obscenities and some yelling worse. Doc Humby smashes his gavel against the podium to get order.

"You sit down Buck! Dr. Klopfenstein administered her new vaccine on my recommendation, and with Thelma Lou's consent. You've had two kids dead from the Spanish flu, do you want a third?"

Humby's eyes move from Buck to the others in the audience, his voice pleading, as Spangler takes his seat. "Mae has given the vaccine to only three patient volunteers," adds the GP, "that was only yesterday. Nellie is one."

"The vaccine is dangerous! No one else has ever heard of it!" screams Prudence as she springs up again, marching over to stand in front of Mae. She wags her finger menacingly at Dr. Klopfenstein. "You're a *witch*!" Her hateful eyes search the others around her. "You hear me, that's what she is: a witch."

Several in the audience also shout out "witch." Then, it turns into a flood of denunciation. The besieged doctor folds her arms in defiance, staring the librarian right in the eye.

"Prudence, you're a learned woman. I'm surprised at you. Shame! The vaccine is *not* dangerous. You're just close-minded. You also don't appreciate the role women can play in furthering medical science," she admonishes.

Ned, outraged by the goings on in the meeting, stands up from his chair, his voice bellowing throughout the auditorium. "How dare you call her a witch? She's a *genius*. Ever hear of Pasteur? Where would mankind be if everyone was as bone-headed as you are, Prudence?"

Prudence retreats to her chair as Ned's pleading eyes roam the other naysayers, "Give the lady a chance, please. As far as her credentials are concerned, it's common practice for some doctors—especially serving in rural areas—to study by correspondence and externships. I've interviewed several."

Spangler's booming voice cuts through the din of the meeting as he stands, pointing his accusatory finger at Mae from his seat. "Miss! You lie! That shot you give 'taint safe!"

"Yes it is," shouts Mae. "I expected this. I'll prove it."

Just then, Ned witnesses the most sensational thing he's ever seen in his life. His heart thumps. Mae takes something out of the pocket of her lab coat. She then unbuttons the top of her coat and blouse right there in front of everybody, and pulls the clothing down from her shoulder, revealing *bare* skin in front of all those strangers! Gasps erupt from the audience.

Mae holds up the object for all to see. To Ned, it looks like a syringe with a needle attached to its end.

"You see this? This is the vaccine," shouts Mae. She then sticks the needle into her arm, pushing down on the plunger with her thumb, draining the contents of the syringe right into her bloodstream. A few screams reverberate throughout the room.

Dr. Humby's eyes expand almost to fill his whole face. "Dr. Klopfenstein, you don't need to do that!"

It is too late. She already did, realizes Ned.

Complete silence fills the large room as the townsfolk stare at the young doctor, as if expecting her to die any second. Mae just stands there, pulling her clothing up to cover her shoulder again, smiling as if she were in the Fourth of July parade. And, after a few minutes of total silence pass, and the people see that Mae is just fine, they seem to realize—*proof positive*— that the doctor's new vaccine is harmless.

Ned claps his hands, shouting: "here, here!"

Presently, the whole auditorium applauds. Mae nods her head in acknowledgement, beaming like the North Star.

Ned realizes with relief that Mae's won the townsfolk over. He also realizes that she's the first woman practitioner in Utah to grace the profession of medicine, right here in good old Shagwood.

* * *

"I thought you might like some company. It's been a while, hasn't it Mae? About five or six months I think, since the town meeting."

Ned Carter sits in front of Dr. Klopfenstein's large mahogany desk, glancing out her office window that showcases the spring-blooms of pink carnations and yellow roses on this glorious but cool, sunny afternoon. "I thought you might like to grab a late lunch."

"I didn't expect you, Ned. I still have a couple of patients—"

"I didn't mean to intrude."

"Not at all. In fact, now that you're here, why don't you let me give you a vaccine shot? I don't think you've had one yet."

Ned puts up his hand and smiles. "Didn't Doc Humby tell you? I can't. I almost died from an injection. Thank you for looking out for me, though. Mae, I just have to tell you that I have the highest regard for you—affection even—"

"Give me an hour. Do you want to wait? Or meet me at the Shagwood Inn? I like the food there."

Ned is disheartened by her interruption, showing little interest in his personal feelings for her. "I'll be in the waiting room." He notices that, by a slight narrowing of her eyes, she's irritated that he didn't choose the option of waiting for her at the hotel. "I'll be thumbing through the *Saturday Evening Post*," he adds.

Just then, Edna pops her head through the cracked door, her manner apologetic. "Sorry Dr. Klopfenstein, but Doc Humby says to remind you that can refer your obstetrics cases to him."

Mae glares at the receptionist, "I prefer to do my own deliveries. Dr. Humby and I have already discussed this. I'll attend to my terminal cases too. This is important for my research . . ."

Mae, somewhat embarrassed by the misunderstanding, stands up from her desk, forcing a smile. "That will be all, Edna." Edna closes the door.

"Where were we now, Ned?'

He notices that Mae's white lab coat now displays her name embroidered in black thread, near her lapel. Her dress and manner look just like her office, muses Ned: attractive, professional, well tended, and little hint of the person to whom it belongs. He wonders if she and old Doc Humby are at loggerheads. Oh well, he realizes, there's no getting away from at least some office politics.

Mae opens the door for Ned. "Until three then," she adds without a smile. I'll meet you in the waiting room. She quickly disappears from the hallway into a patient exam room as Ned files back to the lobby.

On the way, he sees the Heidler girl—Jenny—being led into an exam room by the receptionist. She has a broad smile on her face and a prominent bulge in her lower abdomen. *Poor Jenny's been trying to get pregnant for years, and all hope was lost.* Now, she's expecting, Ned marvels. *Mae must really be a magician.*

He files into the waiting room, taking a chair by the door. He grabs the magazine off the coffee table. On the cover is the title of the feature story: WHAT'S AFTER THE AEROPLANE? SPACE TRAVEL?

Lost in his reading, Ned looks up when a young boy and his mother walk through the door from the back office into the waiting room. He can smell the alcohol on the breath of the woman even at that distance. The boy runs over to Ned and grabs his hand. "Howdy Mr. Carter. Nice to see you! I want you to know that I read that article of yours in the newspaper, sir, and I think it's *erudite* and witty."

Ned is floored. Tommy Jenkins! *What on earth!* Ned glares up at the mother.

She glares back at him. "Leave him alone! My boy's just had another one of those shots from Dr. Klopfenstein. The one for the flu—he don't need any more excitement."

Mrs. Jenkins, looking disheveled in her old, stained, and faded dress, jerks her son by the hand and drags him out the door.

"Goodbye, Mr. Carter," blurts the lad as he nods toward the magazine. "Don't miss the passages about how the moon influences the tides."

Ned's astonished eyes trace the path of the strange patient out the front door. He throws down his magazine and rubs his chin.

My God, he gasps, *what on earth happened to that little Jenkins boy!*

* * *

"I'm impressed with the Jenkins boy," says Ned over his shrimp cocktail. "And Jenny, the Heidler girl—married to George Butts the butcher—she's *finally* pregnant. Odd that I didn't hear about it before, don't you think? You must be doing something right, Mae. Last time I was in the library, old fussbudget Prudence assured me that 'George is as dry as a gourd'.

Mae dabs at her pot roast, her careful eyes scouring Ned over a late lunch, not a speck of a smile on her beautiful face. "Where—oh—you saw them at my office."

"Of course," responds Ned, not expecting her to react so dryly to his good-natured complement and ribald comment about the librarian. "And, I guess they had it wrong about Tommy Jenkins too."

"Do you mean that he's *simple*? Actually, I suspected it was something else all along," Mae interjects quickly while fanning herself. She looks around the dining room. "The windows are open. I wonder why it's so warm in here?"

Ned considers the weather to be a bit on the cool side, but says nothing. "Tommy seemed none too bright to me until today. Tell me more."

Mae puts down the fan and picks up her fork. She eats small bits of her salad. "No fair telling, Ned, there's such a thing as 'patient—doctor privilege'," she says with a pat smile.

"No, really," insists Ned. "I can't believe it. Tell me."

Mae looks at Ned doubtfully, seemingly weighing her options. "All right then; if you must know. On the father's side, there's a history of depression throughout his family tree. The boy's father had it. Tommy was depressed and that can interfere with cognitive function, if severe. That's why he seemed low in intelligence."

"Speak English."

"I gave him a few sessions of psychotherapy. Now he's his real self—brilliant."

"What's that treatment called? *Psycho—*"

"*Psychotherapy,* its from Vienna."

"Never heard of it—"

"Well, you're not a doctor," says Mae with some defensiveness.

Ned polishes off his shrimp salad, silent all the while, mulling over this astounding woman's mark on Shagwood. There's the Jenkins boy, and then there's the progress with Jenny's pregnancy. And, most notable, there's the vaccine.

And, last month, he had heard from Sheriff Mica that Henry Castleton—the truant and PE flunkey, had blossomed into a star athlete and pupil—a model young citizen in fact! Next year he's off to study in Berlin at the Kaiser Wilhelm Institute, where Professor Einstein is working on the relationship between matter and massive amounts of energy. Science journals speculate that it's enough energy to maybe produce enough electricity to light New York City, or even to concoct a monster bomb someday.

Come to think of it, ruminates Ned, Nellie Spangler, the girl who was one of the first patients to benefit from Mae's vaccine, is said to have some great things going on with her about her university plans. Her mother said that she got into some fancy school in Europe, where they study things called '*rockets*' and '*jet propulsion*'.

There's just one thing, Ned realizes with puzzlement. Mr. Jenkins—Tommy's father—now deceased, used to be a good friend of Ned's father. *We knew the family well. Mr. Jenkins never knew his father—Tommy's paternal grandfather. How would Tommy's mother know about this? And, Tommy's father—by all appearances—was a happy man— not depressed at all,* Ned recalls.

Oh well, there must be some simple explanation for this apparent discrepancy, he thinks.

"Mae, I heard that your vaccine program is going like gangbusters. Doc Humby says that the cases of Spanish Flu have dropped significantly. No problems either. He said something about a little tummy upset—that's all."

"Yes Ned, the incidence of the disease has in fact almost gone to zero."

"How many patients of yours get this vaccine now?"

Mae drops her spoon on the floor, then retrieves it. "My, you *are* inquisitive."

"I'm just impressed, that's all," Ned says. "The terrible flu seems to be subsiding—in Shagwood anyway—and I'm very impressed."

"Ned, would you like to go to the Spring Ball with me?" As she abruptly changes the subject, Mae's voice takes on a softness and lilt that Ned hadn't experienced before. "I want to thank you for sticking up for me at the town meeting in December. That was sweet of you."

Then, Mae reaches her arm across the table and gently takes Ned's hand in hers. Ned's caught a bit off guard. "I just don't like to see a newcomer abused," he responds. He removes his hand.

Mae's personal gesture seems forced to Ned, as if he's being manipulated for some reason. A few days ago, Ned would have given a more compelling reason for defending Mae Klopfenstein—a romantic one, in fact—but now, he's not as inclined.

Prudence is right, something's not quite right, he feels.

* * *

A month later, just before the Spring Ball, Prudence Adams marches into Ned's cubicle at the *Gazette*, and plops down in front of his desk as he pecks on his Smith Corona typewriter—completing another feature about meteors. Prudence's face is red, her eyes nervously shifting, and her hands fidgety.

"What's on your mind, Prudence?"

"It's this Dr. Klopfenstein. As the town chronicler and statistician, as well as the librarian, I came across some information that you should know about, Ned. The Utah Public Health Department allowed the doctor to initiate a trail of her vaccine on the condition that she keep a public record of who received the vaccination, and any adverse consequences that may ensue."

"Yes, I know," says Ned as he pushes his typewriter aside and turns his chair toward his tenacious visitor, "Dr. Humby told me about it. In the past six months, she administered to her patients about a hundred vaccinations—mostly to pregnant women and children under eighteen, since they are at high risk for succumbing to the Spanish Flu—"

Prudence pounds her fist on his desk, "*Exactly* Ned, and do you know how many of those *ninety-seven patients* have *died* since then?"

"No, but I'm sure you'll tell me."

"Don't talk to me like that young man. I'm here as a good citizen—"

Ned attempts a smile. "I'm sure you are, but this town has had only three new cases of the flu since the vaccine program started. Before that, we had more than that number every week at least. Now, the announcement from Dr. Humby is official—the flu is totally irradiated in Shagwood."

"Don't change the subject." Mae dips into her huge, flower-embroidered pocketbook and fishes out a couple of papers, throwing them on the desk. "I'm not questioning her competence, I'm questioning her *intent*."

"What?"

"Here, it's documented," she continues. "We had the devil's time getting that data from Dr. Klopfenstein, so I had to do some digging. More than *eleven* out of the ninety-seven patients have died! *Four* young women in childbirth, where the doctor served as the obstetrician herself, *two* children who died of some sort of allergic reaction, where she couldn't save them after they took ill, and *four* children dying in some sort of accident—a few a bit strange, I might add. One patient might have died because they had the flu already—before they took the vaccine—but didn't know it. I saw that one before he died, and he looked *fine* to *me*."

Ned thinks about what she just said, then shakes his head. "I'm no doctor, Prudence. That sounds like a lot, I admit. And, yes, there have been some peculiar things going on in town, I must admit. But I'm sure Dr. Humby knows if anything is out of kilter. He runs the clinic."

Ned leans forward and peers into her eyes, nodding his head. "But, I'm not denying it, these numbers seem strange too, Prudence."

"I'm not saying anything against Doc Humby, mind you," she says. "But I wonder if he knows much about Mae Klopfenstein—"

"You mean like she might be a multiple murderer, like Jack the Ripper, getting her kicks out of knocking off the good citizens of Shagwood one by one?" Ned chuckles. "I think that's going a bit too far."

Prudence's eyes light up. Her lips tighten in into a sliver of a smile. "'Cause you're sweet on the pretty doctor? Hear tell you're taking her to the ball next week."

Ned stands up. "Prudence, I've got work to do."

Ned looks around the cramped and dingy office that smells like ink and oiled presses, deserted except for him and the editor who never leaves his pebbled-glass office across the room. "See this place, Prudence Adams? Not fancy, is it? But, we're proud of it. And we don't go off half-cocked on unsubstantiated tales of serial murder. Good day, Madam."

"Well, I *never* . . . " Prudence springs up from her chair, grabs the papers off the desk and shoves them into her purse, and then marches out of Ned's office.

Ned's stare follows her out the front door. His smile fades and his eyes narrow, lost in thought.

Could she be on to something—something big?

The thought of it horrifies Ned.

* * *

"Is this Dr. Bronfman, the Boston surgeon?" asks Ned as he cocks his ear, sitting at his desk, trying to hear over the latest gadget gracing the world of telephony: the desktop cradle-phone.

Ned can barely hear the response after the short pause, "Yes, it is he."

He can make out a slight accent in the deep, soft voice—probably German. "Doctor, my name is Ned Carter of *The Shagwood Gazette*, and I'm running a feature on our new doctor in town, Mae Klopfenstein—a colleague of Dr. Humby's. She says she studied under you—is that true?"

There's another pause, and then the careful, smooth voice that is slow and precise answers: "Yes, I can say that it is true, although—"

Ned hears the sentence cut off, then nothing. "Doctor, are you still there?" He pushes the cold, gangly object against his face. "Doctor—"

"I am still here."

"Are you familiar with Dr. Klopfenstein's vaccine research?" Ned asks him point blank.

"I *am*. Is this discussion—*private*?"

"Yes, it is."

"I vill only say that her research is extraordinary. *Everything* is extraordinary with her. *That* is precisely the issue."

Ned is confused. He senses that this man is afraid to speak freely. "Give me an example," suggests Ned.

This time there's a longer pause, and Ned hears a sigh on the other end of the phone. "Have you ever heard of the term, '*antibodies*'"?

"What? Can you spell that?"

Bronfman does.

"No, I haven't," responds Ned. "But I'm not a doctor, I'm a newsman."

"Vell, I *am* a doctor—a renowned physician my friend—and I haven't *either*—"

"I don't understand Doctor Bronfman—"

"Nor do I, sir, that is the whole point! I tried to warn Dr. Humby . . ."

Then, there was a click, and the phone went dead.

Confused and upset, Ned puts down the phone, and he stares at the ruler lying on his desk. Not five minutes later the phone rings. He readies himself for grilling the famous Dr. Bronfman further. It must've been a bad connection before, as usual—he surmises.

"Ned, this is Prudence. I've got the goods on the doctor," blurts the librarian in an excited voice, surprising the young reporter. "You meet me at Klopfenstein and Humby's clinic in ten minutes. I'm confronting the doctor with proof—"

"Like what, *specifically*—"

"Just never you mind. I'm the sleuth in charge here. I've got to go now—to pick up some important papers. I'll see you there. Then, we may get Sheriff Mica over there."

The receiver goes dead again, and Ned is even more confused. He knows one thing. Prudence wasn't only excited; she sounded *scared.* Somehow, he feels this time, that Prudence will have the smoking gun—solid evidence of something gone very wrong.

Ned dashes over to Humby's office and waits in the reception room for thirty minutes. He tells the receptionist Edna that he wants to talk to Dr. Humby as soon as he is free.

* * *

"Ned-boy, what can I do for you?" asks Doc Humby.

Ned takes a seat in his office. He clears his throat. "Prudence Adams told me to meet her here at your office—"

The old GP's twinkling eyes narrow, showing concern. "Meet *here*? Why—what's up young fella?" He sits behind his desk, reaching in the drawer for his pouch of tobacco. "She's a handful, isn't she Ned?"

Ned doesn't know what to do, but he decides to just spit it out. "There are a few things going on in town that seem odd to me, too. Even some *medical* things."

"What kind of things?"

"Things concerning Mae Klopfenstein, mostly."

Humby lights his pipe and takes a deep draw on it. "Oh really, like what? You were once her biggest champion—is there something wrong now?"

"The day she comes to town, we have a strange meteor hit. We don't know much of anything about her. I caught her in lie about Tommy Jenkins and his family."

"What lie?"

"I'd rather not get into that now," answers Ned. "Then, your Doctor Bronfman seems to have some strange ideas about Mae."

"Bronfman? When did you talk to him?"

"This afternoon. Prudence also has some documentation—statistics—about Mae's patient base, and what's happened to them since they've received their injections."

"I haven't noticed anything wrong, Ned. What sort of statistics?" Humby blows a blue ring of smoke Ned's way, it hovering over the desk, and then dispersing.

"Eleven of the ninety-seven patients who have received the vaccine have expired, some under questionable circumstances."

Humby frowns. "That does sound like a lot." He empties his pipe in the ashtray. "Statistics can be tricky, Ned. What *questionable* circumstances?"

"You can ask Prudence—by the way—I wonder where she is. She should be here by now." Ned stands up. His eyes fasten on Humby's. "Have you ever heard of a fellow named 'Rudinski'?"

"No," Humby answers, getting to his feet as well.

"How about Dr. Boris Pavlov? They have some theories about a meteor—"

"A meteor, Ned?"

Ned can see that Humby thinks he is getting into left field. He notices a glint of incredulity in his eyes and in his voice. "What does this have to do with our patient outcomes?"

Ned feels flushed. "Well—I don't know, *exactly*—"

Humby comes around the desk and reassuringly pats Ned on the shoulder. "Tell you what, Ned-boy, I'll look over the patient charts—both Mae's and mine—and look into this?"

"Thank you Doctor, I'm sorry to have barged in here, you must've been busy." Ned heads for the door.

Humby opens it for him. "No, not at all, and if the numbers look questionable in any way, rest assured I'll get to the bottom of it."

"Dr. Humby, are you going to the spring ball tomorrow night?"

"Heavens no, Ned. I'm too old for that. You and Mae should have a good time, though. She's looking forward to it. Why do you ask?"

"Nothing really, I just wondered if she had mentioned it."

Ned leaves the office and heads for home on foot, not a quarter mile away. He frets that he came off sounding like a fool to Dr. Humby—or worse—like a lunatic.

One main question shoots through his head, however: why didn't Prudence Adams show up at his office?

* * *

The next evening, the spring ball finally arrives, and Ned sits at one of the better tables, across from Mae Klopfenstein. The Town Hall auditorium is decorated with dim, romantic lights and Japanese lanterns.

An orchestra plays popular tunes on the stage, and, in the corner across the room, sits a refreshment table replete with champagne, little meatballs with toothpicks sticking out of them, a dozen kinds of cheeses sliced into little squares, and non-alcoholic punch for the town's teetotalers, which comprises most of the citizenry. It not being a formal affair this year—in observance to the Spanish Flu victims—no main course is provided, but heaps of napkins, utensils, and little paper plates sit in piles in its place.

"I'm glad you asked me to this affair, Ned," Mae says in a soft, delicate voice, her eyes radiant and warm. This transformation surprises Ned, or maybe it doesn't for that matter, depending upon what she's after. After all, she could be manipulating him. Sadly, Ned thinks that this woman—so gifted in some ways—may be hiding her incompetence.

"Think nothing of it, Mae," Ned responds in a neutral voice as he sips his champagne, eyeing her clothing. She wears a white sweater over a black dress with a necklace—one that is mostly covered up with her sweater. Her dark hair falls down to her shoulders in large curls, which somehow looks unsuitable to her.

Ned chose to wear his dark suit and blue bowtie, over a white, heavily starched dress-shirt. His attire makes him feel just as uncomfortable as the company. "Have you heard the news about Prudence Adams?" asks Ned.

"Yes, yes, I have as a matter of fact. I'm sorry she's dead. Doctor Humby said that she had a massive heart attack. Mae looks around the room, ignoring her glass of champagne, with no change of expression. "Speaking of Dr. Humby," she continues, "I have good news. I'm taking over his practice in one month—*mostly* that is—except for his emergencies and delivery cases. He still wants to be the coroner, but I'm working on that, too. He says he wants to work on his hobbies and keep a hand in my research."

Ned takes another gulp of his drink. "How nice for you. You'll be in control of quiet a bit then, won't you?" Ned had heard the news about Prudence, and this adds to his bewilderment about what the deuce is going on. Now—to his dismay—he hears that Mae will soon be in almost total charge of the clinic.

"I suppose it's natural that Humby slow down, considering what happened. He's getting on in years," Mae says in a throwaway style.

"*Happened*?" Ned's gaze meets her eyes—which are now more serious. "What do you mean? *What* happened?"

Buck Spangler suddenly appears in front of their table, his eyes consumed with rage, his dirty clothes, and breath, reeking of alcohol. He wobbles on his feet as he points his finger at Mae.

"Murderer! *Bitch!* She done killed my baby."

A half-dozen men rush up to restrain Buck as Ned jumps to his feet, putting his hand up to Mr. Spangler to diffuse the situation. "Buck, steady on!"

Spangler drops to his knees, and starts to sob.

The orchestra stops playing. The men help him up and escort him to the door. There's stone silence in the room, and everyone is standing at their tables, staring at Ned and his date. Slowly, people go about their business and resume the festivities as Ned takes his seat, frozen in silence.

"I thought you knew about Jenny," Mae says in almost a whisper as she seats herself too, "Jenny Heidler miscarried, so I hear. She's expired just this morning; seems that it's been quite a week, hasn't it Ned?"

"But she was *your* patient."

"Yes, she was, but Dr. Humby's very upset anyway. He handled the emergency. I didn't want him to, but he did anyway. He wants me to perform an autopsy."

"Why an autopsy?"

"I don't know Ned, she just bled out and she was gone. I said I would. I guess he wants to rule out any other causes of her death."

Mae removes her cashmere sweater. What Ned sees nearly knocks him off his chair. His mind races as his mouth goes dry. He chugs a big gulp of champagne.

Ned's startled eyes are glued on the necklace. It has a gold chain, with a strange pendant at the end, dangling just below Mae's smooth neck.

The pendant is triangular, flat, and smooth, with a strange, vibrant, teal-like color. It's a smaller version of the metallic object that he saw in the meteor crater, and in the old photograph. One question screams into his mind.

What on earth does this all mean?

This seems to connect Mae not only with some strange deaths, but also what Prudence had been talking about and what he had discovered in the library.

Ned leans over the table, closer to his mysterious companion. His voice is gritty and low. "Tell me Mae, what are you really up to with those vaccines?"

Mae just stares at him, saying nothing. She is not even curious about this question. Finally, she answers with a trace of arrogance in her tone. "You're tired tonight, aren't you Ned? You know, maybe I shouldn't tell you this, but I heard about your terrible bouts of depression. Sometime, you can share more of that with me."

Speechless, Ned rises from his chair, claims an acute sickness in his stomach, and quickly escapes the party alone, putting distance between him and Dr. Mae Klopfenstein—the alluring woman in his life who had turned out to be his foulest nightmare.

Part Three

After sitting on a park bench for about an hour, trying to make sense of it all, Ned is walking back to his small apartment overlooking Main Street when he sees another huge flash over Lonely Mountain. There's a deafening sound—this time not a hum—but a noise that sounds like metal scraping metal. Then, there's a huge explosion with an orange fireball, just as before.

He can see people filtering out of their homes, wondering what happened. Ned dashes up to Maple Street to the end of the cobblestone road, where it turns into the trail to the mountain. As he walks up to the L-shaped crest, he sees that the fireball has largely dissipated—the harsh sound is gone.

After hiking a few hundred yards more, he sees a woman walking in front of him, lit up by the half-moon and bright stars. Her white sweater shines in the moonlight. It's Mae Klopfenstein, probably, he figures, on her way to strategize with whatever creatures landed from outer space, blasting their way under the Earth's crust.

She must be one of *them*, he concludes, but why, and *how*?

Ned looks up into the crest of the mountain, observing the dunes and freshly molten rock. This time, there's no evidence of a new crater. The old crevice is gone. Mae just stands there and then disappears, into one of the huge sand dunes, probably—Ned figures—entering a portal to an alien vehicle or outpost buried deep within the mysterious mountain.

Yes, *alien* vehicle, Ned realizes, since a meteor can't hit the same exact place on the Earth's surface twice in a row, especially within just months of each other.

These presumed meteor crashes are really acts of a planned invasion—created by super-intelligent and powerful beings—certainly not humans. The thing that crashed into the mountain came from the sky! *What else could they be but creatures from outer space, like Mr. Wells writes about?*

Ned can't believe that he's thinking this rot, but there it is. He retreats from the mountain. On his way back to his apartment to fetch his revolver, and then on to Humby's house where he'll confront Mae right in front of her esteemed colleague, Ned mulls over the details of these incredible developments, and what to do about it. He wants to get his story straight in front of the old GP, who already thinks that he's loosing his grip.

He'll ring up Humby, and tell him that the three of them must meet immediately—that it's urgent—and concerns life or death issues. If Humby refuses, he'll threaten to go to Sheriff Mica. When they do meet, he'll shoot Mae point blank right in her pretty head. Maybe she can't be killed that way, or at all for that matter, but it's worth a try considering the stakes.

Well, *isn't* it?

Humankind's survival is at state!

As Ned proceeds with his plan, he tries to put all the pieces of the puzzle together. Mae was probably forced to leave her planet, due to climatic changes or other environmental threats. In fact, she seemed overly sensitive to heat, and therefore her planet may be getting too hot to support the creatures living on it. She must know how to change her appearance and to conform to Earthling standards, being from an advanced, super-intelligent civilization.

Ned has a clear picture now of what's going on. Mae had injected the seed of an alien creature into humans by way of the vaccine, so the aliens could incubate, and then be extracted somehow while Mae claimed the hosts had died due to other causes—like childbirth, accident, or illness. The so-called "fetuses" are probably stored in their spaceship, buried deep below Lonely Mountain.

With some younger humans, a true symbiotic relationship was established, where the carrier also had benefited from the implant. Mae had described that process herself in the greenhouse. Tommy, Nellie, and Henry—they all became prodigies in science and technology *after* their injections. With Nellie, Ned speculates, the alien growing inside her had gotten sick, and killed her. Nevertheless, through science and wars, the aliens would make sure that humans murdered each other to extinction. That's where Haber, Einstein, Bronfman, and the Kaiser all contributed to the plan. *Were they carriers, or merely patsies,* Ned wonders? Actually—in a perverse way—he could see how, given the Earth's bleak history, the fact of human collaborators isn't surprising.

Ned finally arrives at his apartment, opens the door to his study, and retrieves his Colt revolver from the desk drawer. He then calls Humby.

"Doctor, it's Ned Carter. I have a life-or-death problem that's come up. I need to meet you and Mae Klopfenstein at your office—within a half-hour . . . yes, it's something grave . . . yes, it's urgent! If we can't resolve this ourselves, I'm going to Sheriff Mica . . . no, I don't have time to tell you now . . . thank you, good-bye."

Ned hangs up, puts on his heavy coat over his suit coat, stuffs his revolver into its deep pocket, and then heads out for the good doctor's home.

He's ready to destroy Mae Klopfenstein.

* * *

Ned stands in front of Dr. Humby, the old GP bending over his prized plants in the greenhouse with his watering can in his chubby little hands. "What's the problem, Ned, you look troubled my boy."

"Where's Mae?" Ned asks.

"She'll be here directly; probably in a few minutes. I left the front door open. She's concerned about you, Ned, especially since you left her so abruptly at the spring ball. She said that you looked wild—*raving* in fact. Are you feeling better? How about your sleep lately?"

Ned moves close to Humby, facing him, and the door to the greenhouse behind him. One hand grips his gun, planted deep within his overcoat pocket. His legs ache and his head is on fire with emotions and horrific facts. He looks his old friend in the eye, gathering up the courage to explain to him the most insane, unearthly tale anyone's ever heard of, and all about his dear colleague Dr. Mae Klopfenstein.

"You see, it's like this, Doctor Humby, in short—your associate—Dr. Klopfenstein—I can prove all this if you just hear me out—is an *alien* from outer space—uh, with her invasion force camping inside Lonely Mountain. She's planning to take over the Earth . . . using her vaccines mind you . . . yes, furthermore, she murdered Prudence Adams to keep her quiet—"

"I see, Ned, very interesting," says Humby as he puts down the watering can.

"You mean you *believe* what I'm telling you."

The congenial doctor removes his pipe and tobacco pouch from his coat pocket, and fills the pipe as he talks in his smooth voice. "You live alone Ned; you're lonely for someone to confide in. You've been working hard. We all have our breaking point—"

"But Doctor Humby, she's been filling her vaccine with alien seeds, to sew our destruction—mankind's extinction!"

"Ned-boy, please—"

Ned realizes how crazy he sounds, but he has no choice. "The world is in jeopardy!" he screams. "Good God, man, can't you see this?"

Humby puts the pouch back in his pocket, then lights his pipe. "Your mental disorder is flaring again, Ned-boy—"

Ned takes a step forward, his eyes ablaze. "Just listen to me!"

The good doctor takes a deep draw on his pipe, his eyes rolling over his beloved plants. He let's out a deep sigh, but says nothing.

"Is Mae really meeting us here?" asks Ned.

"No. I told her about how upset you seemed over the phone, and about what you said when we met last—about *her*—I mean. I told her to stay home."

"I'm going to Sheriff Mica, Dr. Humby, someone needs to take me seriously before it's too late!"

Humby smiles, blowing smoke rings at Ned. He points his pipe at him. "Oh, but I *do* take you seriously, my boy, very seriously. Let me show you something."

Humby reaches over to a pole that has wires running up it, and flips a light-switch. The greenhouse goes completely dark. Ned sees that the plants—especially the big ones that now look like *giant* eggplants—are phosphorescent and writhing—with some sort of strange creature housed within the plant's slimy, transparent skin, making noises that sound like a dog whimpering.

Humby turns the lights back on, and the eerie glow from the plants disappears, as does the noise.

Ned is stunned. He can't believe his eyes. "It was *you* all along, not *her*."

"You're spot on, Ned. You see you had the situation right, but the wrong *person*."

Ned is speechless. He fingers the trigger of his hidden gun.

"Yes indeed," continues Humby, "I hired Mae to be my patsy. She thought she was injecting flu sera, but all along I laced the normal saline with my seeds—the essence of *my* civilization."

Humby laughs. "I've been doing this on and off for a hundred years—not just here—but other places too. I'm sure you heard of Siberia. My greenhouse is where I store our '*infants*'—a kindergarten, so to speak—cut out of the innards of the human hosts. As coroner and mortician, I covered my tracks nicely."

"Then, the first meteor was your spaceship—more of your people invading us," Ned says, hoping that his gun-blast is enough to kill this creature standing before him. "What about that strange metal object within the crevice?"

"It's a special form of energy for our kind—to preserve our life-force, as it were. I guess it is closest to what your kind calls a 'battery'."

"But Mae wore one, at the ball—"

"I gave it to her so that she would wear it near me. If *I* wore it, it would look too strange for an old, ugly codger like me. Well, you should see how ugly I am in my *real* form." Humby laughed at that one. "Of course, Mae knew nothing about this."

"What about the *second* meteor?" Ned asks, both revolted and fascinated by this strange trip through science and outer space.

Humby has no answer for that one, just a frown. He flicks his ashes from the pipe on the floor, and puts the cold pipe in his pocket. "Maybe that one was *really* a meteor."

Ned is frozen, numb to everything except the fear of the nightmare that engulfs him.

"I hate to do this Ned. For a human, you're very likable."

Dr. Humby retrieves a pistol from his pocket—the same one that had been in his desk drawer—and aims it at Ned. "Guns are dangerous for our kind too, so I must use care. I don't like crazy patients barging into my house, threatening me—especially ones with a past of mental instability. That's exactly what I'll explain over your body after I phone Sheriff Mica—telling him to get over to here immediately."

Ned sees the door behind Humby slowly open, and Mae Klopfenstein appears. She has a gun too, but it's aimed at Humby, not him. He figures that she just decided to come over anyway, sensing that the old GP may be in danger. A pang of guilt shoots through him for blaming her for all the strange things that had been going on.

Humby moves closer to Ned, aiming his gun straight for Ned's heart. "As for Mae, she's served her purpose. Soon, I'll liquidate *her* too. She's getting too controlling anyway. Good-bye, Ned, have a good trip—"

"Not so fast, Humby," says Mae. There's a loud explosion from Mae's smoking gun.

Humby disintegrates into a display of incredibly colorful fireworks, some colors Ned had never seen before. The colored lights fade fast, and then there's nothing left of old Doc Humby. The force of the bullet must've been enough to obliterate the creature, Ned figures with relief.

Ned rushes over to embrace Mae, kissing her wildly on the mouth. She drops the gun. "I love you, Mae!" He begs her to forgive him for doubting her, when she was innocent all along, and tells her that he's eternally grateful to her for saving not only his life, but also perhaps the world. He kisses her again—wet kisses . . .

Then, Ned feels a sharp, horn-like object jet into his mouth. He steps back, and Mae is shedding her exterior shell of human flesh and clothing, metamorphosing into a creature that looks like a cross between a jellyfish and a horned ape.

As she speaks, her soft voice slowly transforms into a tinny, metallic sound. "No Ned, I *wasn't* innocent. Yes, I'm from another planet too, only Venus, not Mars like him. We studied symbiotic relationships too, and discovered what Humby was doing on Earth. Symbiotic infiltration is the key to successful colonization."

Ned, stunned, can barely find words. "What about the explosion on the mountain tonight? You were there—"

"The first meteor was Humby's spacecraft," echoes the metallic voice, "the second was *ours*—taking over. We store our fledgling aliens there now. I snuck in here this morning and poisoned Humby's infants here in the greenhouse. By tomorrow, there'll be unviable. Humby knew nothing about my real purpose and my origins, and I stole his technology for the survival of *our* race. We are advanced Ned, and patient, and we will—"

"Suppose I tell everyone about this. Suppose I inform the sheriff, or even the US Army in Washington." Ned backs up a few steps, the unsightly creature giving off a powerful odor, a much stronger version of the perfume that she had worn before.

The transformation being complete, the alien creature's voice is nearly unintelligible. "Who is going to believe you?" asks the creature. "I suggest that you take the vaccine. Allergy will not be a problem. Take it, and become one of us, like your pal Flash. You can achieve for us great advances in science. I'm revealing my real self to you because this is my hope. I've—always found you attractive, Ned dear. You know you want to . . ."

Ned reaches into his coat pocket and draws his gun. He discharges it into what's left of Mae's human head. It's too late. The horns and the slime had turned into thousands of pixilated dots, rising to the ceiling, evaporating into thin air.

Ned takes a deep breath, letting it out, and then wipes the sweat from his forehead. His mind races: even if that creature's dead, which it probably isn't, he must now lay plans to warn the world of the apocalyptic danger—and fast.

But, how can we fight them, Ned asks himself? *Who would believe me in the first place? They'd lock me up in an asylum. Will humans just march to their own destruction no matter what I say or do?*

He puts his gun away, and plops down on a wooden plant-box, cradling his head in his hands. He sees the plants in the greenhouse shriveling away, making horrible, groaning sounds as they die.

Ned thinks about his future, and the power and intelligence of Mae and her race. He then shakes his head and looks up at the silhouette of Lonely Mountain, dark and mysterious through the glass ceiling.

He mutters to himself, "Maybe I'll join her after all—and *them*— and see what kind of world *they* can offer."

END OF NOVELETTE THREE

AFTERWORD

In our first novelette, legendary disasters like the Donner Party or the Titanic, or, our Crawler Party—if you will—may not just happen and then leave history to fill in the cracks. The uncanny, violent deaths of hundreds of people due largely to fate may trigger mystic shockwaves far into the future, where unsavory forces play out their final act of revenge or destiny. Something compelled Sylvia Crawler to consummate the grisly acts of her forbears, her heritage serving as a grim tool to satisfy a primitive lust for retribution. If we had gotten into the mind of Black-Tongue more, would he have been sympathetic to the Crawlers, or join in damning them? The Donner Party—that did in fact meet tragedy when failing to traverse a snowed-in pass—experienced cannibalism and other grisly acts. Could their spirits still be wandering the mountains around Tahoe?

In our second story, we peered into the lonely lives of a new race of robots, who, along with the human-like gift of intelligence—even super-intelligence—inherited, through astounding feats of applied science, very human *flaws* as well: egomania, greed, and aggression. Will we breed a race of machines that will ultimately rebel against us, like Dorian did? Will the story of Spartacus and his gladiators, who turned on their ancient Roman masters, play out again? Will we create electronic brains that will ultimately cast off their role as menials and seize a dark independence, hunting humankind like cockroaches? As the human brain evolved, it acquired the excess capacity to not only ward off beasts lurking within trees or caves, but to savagely and efficiently kill off other humans as well, eventually by the millions. Will robots have their own nefarious evolution? We may want robots to love us, but does that mean they must be able to *hate* as well? The future may hold for us what it held for Dorian and the others, unless we build in safeguards to prevent free will from evolving into grisly slaughter.

Our last tale also presents humankind with a bleak challenge. Webster's Dictionary defines the word "symbiosis" as the intimate living together of two distinct organisms that experience mutual advantage from their association. Will invaders from outer space conquer us with powerful spaceships and cataclysmic missiles and then colonize what is left? Or, will they use their superior intelligence and patience to accomplish this task with far more finesse and stealth, inheriting an Earth that is not despoiled by their advanced level of combat?

Perhaps, as in our story, they will use a beloved practitioner to introduce their Trojan horse: Dr. Mae Klopfenstein and her vaccine. She did indeed embrace symbiosis, where some humans at first *do* benefit from the alien organism introduced into their bodies. This "benefit," of endowing the host with an aptitude for more advanced scientific achievement, also sews the seeds—through more advanced weaponry—of humankind's self-destruction, thus benefiting the aliens in the end. Too bad for Dr. Humby—who had the same goal for *his* kind—that he was outfoxed by Mae.

If you enjoyed this, please write an online review on Amazon or Audible.com.

END OF BOOK ONE OF *PURPLE MIST* SERIES: MORE BOOKS PLANNED